ANDI UNDER PRESSURE

Other books by Amanda Flower

Appleseed Creek Mystery Series

A Plain Death

A Plain Scandal

A Plain Disappearance

India Hayes Mystery Series

Maid of Murder

Murder in a Basket

Amish Quilt Shop Mystery Series

(writing as Isabella Alan)

Murder, Plain and Simple

An Andi Boggs Novel

Andi Unexpected

AN ANDI BOGGS NOVEL

ANDI UNDER PRESSURE

AMANDA FLOWER

ZONDERKIDZ

Andi Under Pressure
Copyright © 2014 by Amanda Flower

This title is also available as a Zondervan ebook.
Visit www.zondervan.com/ebooks

Requests for information should be addressed to:

Zonderkidz, 3900 *Sparks Dr. SE, Grand Rapids, Michigan 49546*

Library of Congress Cataloging-in-Publication Data

Flower, Amanda.
    Andi under pressure : an Andi Boggs novel / by Amanda Flower.
      pages cm
    ISBN 978-0-310-73702-5 (hardcover) — ISBN 978-0-310-73768-1 (epub) —
ISBN 978-0-310-74022-3 (softcover)
    [1. Practical jokes—Fiction. 2. Science camps—Fiction. 3. Best friends—
Fiction. 4. Friendship—Fiction. 5. Mystery and detective stories.] I. Title.
PZ7.F6676Ams 2014
[Fic]—dc23   2014016557

Cover illustration: Chris Coady
Cover design: Cindy Davis
Interior design: David Conn

Printed in the United States of America

14 15 16 17 18 19 20 /DCI/ 19 18 17 16 15 14 13 12 11 10 9 8 7 6 5 4 3 2 1

For my nephew, Andrew
with all my love

The old man wearing the black leather gloves was back. He sat crossed-legged on the sidewalk and edged the grass with kitchen scissors. Yesterday, on the first day of Discovery Camp, I spotted him digging a hole with a screwdriver. I glanced around. Was I the only person on Michael Pike University's campus that found his choices in garden tools peculiar or just plain weird?

I was used to weird to a point. Usually when I came down to breakfast each morning, my aunt Amelie was standing on her head or in the middle of another yoga contortion. But that was weird in the privacy of our own home. This was weird out in the open.

I studied the man. I guessed that he was about the age of Colin's grandma, Bergita, maybe a little older. Besides the gloves, he wore a gray university work shirt and too-big black jeans held up by a brown belt. His face was so wrinkled that he had slits where his eyes should have been. He wasn't alone. A grizzled beagle that may have been as old as him sat on the sidewalk, watching the man's progress. The beagle buried her nose into the freshly cut grass.

I didn't even know why he bothered to trim the lawn this late in the summer. The blades of grass were scorched by long, hot months with little rain.

Colin Carter, my next-door neighbor and closest friend in Killdeer, chained his bike to the rack outside Colburn Hall, the university's science building. "Dr. Ruggles's lecture yesterday on invertebrates would have been better if he actually let us touch one of his precious samples. Did he think we would drop them? It's not like we haven't picked up a bug before."

I tucked a stray piece of strawberry blond — sadly, closer to pink — hair behind my ear, half-listening to Colin. All my attention was focused on the man and dog. "Colin, who is that?"

Colin struggled with his bike lock. "Who is who?" His floppy brown hair fell over the top of his glasses. He blew it away with a puff of air.

I pointed across the grounds. "That guy. Who is he?"

"Oh, that's Polk," he said. "He works here. I think he's a janitor. I've seen him mopping the bathrooms in Colburn before."

"Is Polk his first name or last name?"

Colin fiddled with the lock's chain. "I don't know. It's what everyone calls him."

"Yesterday was the first time I saw him," I pau[ ] guess that's his dog."

"Oh yeah, that's Curie. I don't think I have ever seen him without Curie. I mean, except when Polk is in one of the buildings cleaning or fixing stuff." Colin shrugged.

I frowned. "What's with the scissors?"

Colin straightened up and squinted at the man. "Maybe he couldn't find a Weedwacker."

I folded my arms. "You don't think that's strange he's cutting the grass with kitchen scissors?"

Colin shrugged again. "Bergita says he's a good egg."

Colin lived with his grandmother, Bergita. He always called her by her first name. Everyone did.

"How does Bergita know Polk?" I asked.

"Bergita knows everyone."

I studied Polk more closely. His shoulders hunched forward as he worked. Curie sniffed around a lamppost.

I was about to question Colin more about Polk when Dylan White, wearing his blue Discovery Camp counselor T-shirt, jogged toward Colin and me. "Hey, you two, what are you doing out here?" He ran a hand through his perfectly wavy brown hair. "Camp is about to start." Dylan was a sophomore chemistry major and cross-country star. He could also rap the periodic table. Yesterday, he'd done it twice.

Colin slung his backpack over his shoulder. "Andi was asking about Polk."

Dylan glanced over to Polk and back to me. "Andi, you are destined to be a great scientist because you question *everything*."

I fought the blush creeping across my cheeks.

9

He flashed his megawatt smile. "That's not a bad thing, but you don't need to worry about Polk. He's harmless. Weird but harmless." Dylan grimaced.

At least someone else thought Polk's actions were weird.

"Let's go, kids. You don't want to be late for opening, do you? If you are, you'll have to answer to Madison."

Madison Houser was the upperclassman in charge of Discovery Camp. She took her job *very* seriously and would not put up with any "shenanigans." At least that's what she told us yesterday. She'd actually said "shenanigans" with a straight face too.

"Kids," Colin snorted. "You're not *that* much older than us."

Dylan grinned at Colin's comment. "There is a difference between twelve and nineteen, my friend. I can drive and I can vote. What do you have?"

Colin crossed his eyes at the counselor and was rewarded with a bark of laughter.

Beyond Polk and Curie, Madison marched across the green carrying a huge stack of lab manuals. Her brown ponytail bounced with each step which didn't seem to match the scowl on her face.

Dylan dashed across the lawn and took the lab books from Madison's arms. She gave him a tight smile. Dylan returned it with a big goofy grin like the ones I had seen on Colin's pug, Jackson, when Bergita was about to give him a Milk-Bone. Madison just scowled harder and marched into the building with Dylan a few steps behind.

Colin headed for Colburn's front doors. "We're

going to be late for opening. I don't want to start today with a lecture from Madison, do you?"

No way, I thought. I took one last glance at Polk and Curie. The old man was still seated on the sidewalk. He turned his head and nodded at me.

"Andi!" Colin held the door open for me.

I ran inside.

CASE FILE NO. 2

Colin and I fell into our chairs in Colburn's lecture hall just as Madison began to take the roll. "Boggs!" she called in a surprisingly husky voice.

"Here!" I piped up, hoping I didn't sound out of breath.

Madison made a check on her clipboard. Madison loved her clipboard. Another student asked to see it on the first day, and she'd ripped it from his hands. No one messed with the clipboard.

Madison called, "Carter?"

"Present," Colin squeaked.

Dylan stood behind Madison and pretended to write a check mark on an imaginary clipboard. The thirty-two kids in the classroom and the other counselors, Luis and Susan, tried not to laugh.

Madison's eyes narrowed. She whipped her head around to face Dylan. He wiggled his fingers at her.

The class couldn't hold back any longer. We burst into giggles.

"No more fun and games. Science is serious business," Madison snapped.

Because of her small size, it was like watching a mouse snarl. I covered my mouth. She would *hate* that comparison.

Madison glared at each one of us in turn. Her eyes lingered on me longer than the rest. "Break up into your element groups," she said finally, "and your counselor will escort you to your first class for the day. At the end of the day, we will reconvene in this room for a recap and closing. Any questions?"

"What college student says 'reconvene'?" I heard someone whisper.

Dylan put two fingers in his mouth and whistled. "Yo, Hydrogen over here."

Madison scowled at him. "Helium, please come to the front of the room. Bring your backpacks with you."

Colin and I shared a look. We were both thinking the same thing: we were glad to be in Dylan's, not Madison's, group.

The last two groups, Lithium and Zinc, belonged to Susan and Luis. Luis was quiet and had just the hint of a mustache on his upper lip. I didn't know why he didn't shave it off and wait until he could grow a more respectable one. Susan played basketball for the university and had what Bethany would call a "sporty" build. She ran down the line of her group members and high-fived her students. Some of them winced when her hand hit theirs. She gave her group, Lithium, a lot of high fives, and they were beginning to feel it.

"First up for Lithium is ecology. Who's ready?" The student next to her covered his ears.

I was about to take the seat next to Dylan when Ava Gomez, the only other girl in my element group, slid into the seat beside him, hitting me in the face with her dark ponytail in the process. I spat her hair out of my mouth. Not for the first time, I wished that there were more than eight girls at Discovery Camp. Ava's lab partner Jake, a thin kid with large ears, slumped in the seat next to her. He propped his hand under his chin and blinked half-closed eyes.

Dylan reached over and tapped Jake on the back of his blond head. "Someone didn't eat his Wheaties today, did he?"

Jake yawned.

Ava elbowed him in the ribs. "Wake up!"

Jake straightened up a little, but when Ava turned her attention back to Dylan, he fell back into a slouch. My brow wrinkled. How did they end up as lab partners?

Dylan removed a crumbled piece of paper from his pocket and smoothed it out on the tabletop. "Okay, kids, here's the rest of the lineup. Today, we have chemistry first, then bio, lunch, eco-time, and then free period."

At the front of the room, Madison had a binder that told her where to go and what to do. Even Luis and Susan had folders. Dylan kept his schedule on the back of a crumpled receipt in his jeans' pocket. The other counselors reviewed the camp rules and ongoing projects. Dylan didn't bother with any of that. Ours was the first group to leave.

In the hallway, we heard the hum of classrooms' window air conditioners fighting a losing battle with the heat outside. The interior stairwell was a little bit cooler than the hallway but not by much. When we reached the third floor, Colin wheezed softly. Was his asthma acting up again? I'd witnessed him having an attack once, and one time was enough.

"Do you need to use your inhaler?" I whispered.

He drank from his red Discovery Camp water bottle. "I'll be okay."

We filed into the classroom through the back door and took our spots at the lab tables, but Dr. Comfrey, the chemistry professor, wasn't there. Ava had pushed her way to a seat at the front lab table. She glanced around the classroom with a smug look on her face. The air conditioner dripped water onto the floor under the window.

Dylan grinned and marched to the front of the room. "I suppose I will have to teach lab today. Everyone pull out your Bunsen burners and fire them up. I'll get the propane."

Thump!

"Ow!" a voice cried from under Dr. Comfrey's desk. A second later, Dr. Comfrey's dark curly hair appeared over the top of the desk. She stood, rubbing the back of her head. "That's not amusing, Mr. White. Bunsen burners, as common as they are in a lab, can be dangerous if the person operating them doesn't know how to use them."

"It was a joke." Dylan flashed another megawatt smile.

The chemistry professor untangled her fingers from her brown curls. She was a small woman. I had two inches on her and was still growing. She wore a white lab coat that reached her ankles over a Discovery Camp T-shirt and jeans. Without the coat, she could have passed for one of the kids in her classroom.

"I'm glad to see you are all already at your work stations," she said as she spun her long curls into a bun on the back of her head and secured it into place with two number two pencils.

"Why were you under the desk?" Colin asked.

The petite professor smiled at him. "I misplaced something."

"What did you lose?" Gavin, an African-American boy, asked. He had an atom diagram shaved into the hair on the side of his head. I wondered what Amelie would say if I came home with a hairstyle like that. Knowing my aunt, she'd liked it.

Gavin's mother drove an hour one way to bring him back and forth to camp. I wondered where my other Hydrogen-mates were from. I shot a glance at Ava, who was already taking notes, for what I couldn't guess since class hadn't started yet. I hoped Ava was from another place too, like Siberia, or seventh grade would be what Bergita called a "doosie." I'd ask Colin about her when I got a chance.

The teacher laughed. "I lost all my dry erase markers. There weren't any in the whiteboard well this morning. I could have sworn I left four there last night." She shook her head. "I thought I had a box in the cupboard too. It's so odd that they would all go missing at once." She forced a laugh. "I'm very meticulous about supplies." She smiled at Dylan. "You know that from Chem One, don't you, Dylan?"

"I do." He pressed his lips together into a straight line.

Dr. Comfrey shrugged. "I'm sure they will turn up when I least expect it. Isn't that the way of it?"

"Maybe we can help you look for them," I offered.

Someone near me whispered, "Suck up."

I whipped my head around, but didn't see who it was. Ava would have been my first guess, but it didn't sound like a girl's voice.

"Thank you, Andora." She adjusted the pencils on the back of her head and peered at the class list on her desk. "It is Andora, isn't it?"

I opened my notebook. "You can call me Andi."

"Okay then, Andi, that is a very sweet offer, but you did not come to camp to search for my lost markers. I'll pick some up at the store this evening. In the meantime, Dylan, can you go next door to room 318? There is a rolling chalkboard in there." She smiled. "I've got chalk. We will rock this lecture old school."

"Come on, Spenser." Dylan waved at a husky kid sitting in the back row. "You can help me out."

Dr. Comfrey stopped fussing with her pencils and said, "Let's not waste any more precious class time on lost markers." She laughed. This time it was a true laugh. "Today, we are going to talk about alkalinity. Who knows what an alkaline is?"

I raised my hand. As I did, Ava called out, "An alkaline is a substance that has a pH greater than seven. It is the opposite from an acid which has a pH less than seven."

Dr. Comfrey nodded. "That is correct, Ava, but I wish you would wait for me to call on you before you answer." She peered over Ava's head. "Andi, what more can you tell me about alkalis?"

I cleared my throat. "Because it is the opposite of acid, it can neutralize acid. It's found in many batteries too."

Ava glared at me. Yes, seventh grade would be a ball if she went to my school. Please, no.

"Excellent Andi. It sounds to me as if you have studied them before."

"I've read about them," I admitted.

In the row in front of me, Ava glanced back and whispered to her lab partner Jake. His chuckle turned into a yawn. I stiffened. Spenser and Dylan returned pushing the heavy chalkboard.

"Right here is fine." Dr. Comfrey pointed to the space in front of her white board. "Thanks, guys."

Spenser lumbered back to his seat.

While Dr. Comfrey lectured about alkali and all their uses, I watched Dylan. Quietly, he straightened the chalkboard and walked to the stool in the back of the room. He didn't stop to crack a joke or even a smile. I couldn't help but notice how his posture wasn't that much different than Polk's had been earlier that morning. He wouldn't make eye contact with me or anyone else. Ever since Dr. Comfrey mentioned Chem One, he was deflated.

I turned back around to face the chalkboard and found Ava frowning at me from two rows up.

"What?" I mouthed.

She didn't answer. Instead she spun around in her seat, hitting Jake in the face with her ponytail. I had no idea why, but Ava Gomez was out to get me.

At the end of chemistry, I slid my notebook into my backpack while Colin waited for me by the classroom door.

"Andi?" Dr. Comfrey ran a black eraser across the chalkboard. "Can you stay after class for a moment?"

I swallowed hard. Did Dr. Comfrey know Colin and I had been a few minutes late for opening that morning? I couldn't think of any other reason the chemistry professor would want me to stay behind. But if that were true, wouldn't she have asked Colin to stay too?

Colin raised his eyebrows. I gave him a sideways smile and gestured he should go with Dylan and the rest of Hydrogen to biology. He waited in the doorway for a half second longer and then disappeared down the hall.

My sneakers squeaked on the tile as I shifted my feet in front of her desk.

Dr. Comfrey dusted chalk off of her jeans. "Chalk is terrible stuff. It gets everywhere. I will definitely have to stop at the store for markers tonight."

I murmured that that was a bummer for her, still wondering what she wanted to say to me.

The chemistry professor sat behind her desk. "I asked you to stay after class because I wanted to tell you how excited we are to have you as part of the program this summer. You had the highest test scores in the sciences of those who applied." She stacked a pile of papers on her desk. There was a glossy pamphlet on top. It had a photograph of the Centers for Disease Control and Prevention building in Washington DC on it. "Undergraduate Think Tank" was splashed across the cover above two smiling college students in lab goggles and coats.

I blinked. "I did?" I paused. "What about Colin?"

Colin was the kid genius, not me. I had even heard people in town call him that.

She smiled. "Colin's were the highest overall, but you shone in the sciences."

"Wow," I murmured. My chest constricted. I wished I could tell my parents. Both had been award-winning botanists, but they had died in a plane crash in Central America only a few months ago. I looked down, suddenly feeling a wave of the pain that never really went away.

"I can't tell you how much it excites me. We need more female scientists."

"What about Madison? She's going to be a scientist, isn't she?"

The professor pursed her lips together. "Yes, she is. A gifted one. Just like you. Discovery Camp is very selective with only thirty-two spots for both seventh and eighth graders." She tapped the think tank brochure. "You might be going to this someday. I'm able to recommend one student every year for the program. One of my best students, Fletcher, is there right now. If you follow the path you're going, this could be you in eight or ten years." She frowned. "If the funding for the program comes back, that is. We won't be able to send a student next summer because of budget cuts." She flipped the pamphlet over, hiding the smiling college students' faces. "But enough about that. I'm so glad you applied, and we made an exception to give you a spot even if it was well after the deadline."

I gnawed on the inside of my cheek. The deadline had been April first, but I applied in June. My aunt, who was an English professor at Michael Pike, requested special permission for my application to be considered because Bethany and I had just moved to Killdeer to live with her after the plane crash. If there were only thirty-two spots, that meant I took a spot away from someone who had already earned it.

I glanced at the open door and saw a swish of dark hair pass over the opening. Was that Ava?

The chemistry professor removed her reading glasses and dropped them into one of the huge pockets of her lab coat. "Something wrong, Andi?"

"If only thirty-two kids get into Discovery Camp,

and I applied late, I took somebody's spot." I dug the toe of my sneaker into the leg of her desk.

She shook her head. "We didn't kick anyone out of the camp to let you in, if that's what you are afraid of. The student you replaced gave up his spot even before you applied. Instead of coming to Discovery Camp, he went to spend the summer with his grandparents."

I blew out a sigh of relief.

She sat in her desk chair and opened a drawer. "Now, off to biology with you. Dr. Ruggles will be annoyed with me for keeping you so long." She smiled. "It's my free period now, and I'm going to see if I can track down some dry erase markers."

I thanked her and floated from the room. I had the highest scores in science. Even higher than Colin's. Maybe I *would* be a great scientist someday like both of my parents had been. They died for their careers on a research trip in Guatemala searching for endangered plants.

My tennis shoes squeaked on the waxed tile floors. The hall was empty. Was Dr. Comfrey right? Would I be going to a CDC think tank someday like Fletcher? That would have impressed my parents.

In the middle of the hallway was a glass display case. Behind the glass, there were photographs of three students. I recognized two: Madison and Dylan. There was another boy in between them. He was a nerdy-looking kid. The name "Fletcher Manuel" was beneath his photograph. This was Dr. Comfrey's student who was at the think tank this summer. Above the photographs there was lettering which read, "Our Top Chemistry Students!" Madison was in the first position. Her grade point average was 4.0. Fletcher and Dylan were close behind with 3.85 and 3.8.

A sharp clatter interrupted my thoughts, followed by a gasp. I spun around to face the noise, but no one was there. The dim hallway was empty. I took a step. At the end of the hall, I heard the sound of running footsteps followed by a loud bang like someone threw a book against a locker.

I chased the noise. "Is someone there?"

I skidded to a stop at the end of the hall, where it took a sharp turn and led to another passageway. This one was lined with closed doors with names on them—the science faculty offices, I figured.

The first doorknob I tried was locked. As much as I wanted to try every door, I knew I had to return to Hydrogen. The next lab session already had begun, and stuffy Dr. Ruggles must have noticed my absence by now.

I turned and immediately had the eerie feeling I was being watched. Up and down the hallway, all the doors were shut. A piece of white plastic about the size of my thumbnail lay near my feet. I picked it up but had no idea what it might have belonged to or where it came from. Dropping the piece into my shorts pocket, I ran to the stairwell and took the steps two at a time to the second floor. When I pushed open the heavy stairwell door, I heard shouts coming from the biology lab.

Through the doorway, I saw Dr. Ruggles—who was built like Mr. Potato Head with a thick trunk and skinny arms—crawling on the floor like a baby in a race. His toupee sat off-kilter on the top of his head.

He wasn't the only one on the floor. Half of the class was on all fours too.

"Try not to step on them!" the professor shouted as he fast-crawled around the desk in pursuit of something I couldn't see.

I inched into the room. *Chirp-chirp.* A cricket hopped over my foot.

"Andi, don't let that one get away," the biology teacher ordered.

I bent to scoop up the cricket but was too slow, and it slipped under a lab table.

Colin's foot stuck out from behind a rolling television cart at the back of the lab. Gingerly, I stepped over my crawling classmates to reach him. I was about to ask Colin what was going on when he pounced. "I got one!" His glasses sat crookedly on his nose. He grinned up at me, and another cricket jumped and bounced off his cheek. He swatted at it, and as he did the cricket he'd just caught escaped.

"If I didn't know better, I would say these are mutant crickets, capable of rational thought, who were working together as a team," Colin muttered.

"How did the crickets get out?" I asked.

Colin stood and brushed his hair out of his eyes. "No idea. We came into the lab and Dr. Ruggles was already on the floor gathering crickets by the dozens."

The biology professor's face was dangerously red. I don't think Mr. Potato Head was built for crawling on the floor. Dr. Ruggles crawled to the other side of the room. "Everyone, catch those crickets!"

A few feet away from Colin and me, Ava covered three crickets with a bowl and slipped a piece of paper beneath the bowl. When she flipped the bowl over, the paper was on top and the crickets were trapped inside. She dropped them into a large aquarium with even more crickets. After depositing the crickets, she took her bowl and searched for her next catch.

Jake jumped across his desk and caught another. His camp binder slammed to the floor. I winced to think of any cricket in the binder's path.

"Careful!" was Dr. Ruggles's muffled cry from under his desk

Brady and Chase, the last two members of Hydrogen, crowed when they each trapped a cricket.

Spenser peered under the desk at the biology professor. "Maybe we should let the geckos out. They can catch the crickets for us." He pointed to the aquarium near the classroom door where three geckos lived. I noticed two of them had their faces pushed up next to the glass, watching the action. Maybe they wondered why dinner was on the floor.

"No! Do not let out the geckos." The plump professor struggled to his feet.

"It was just a suggestion," Spenser muttered and resumed the hunt.

Dylan slipped into the classroom. I hadn't noticed he was missing until just then. Where had he been while Group Hydrogen hunted crickets?

The counselor winked at me as he perched on a stool. "I feel like I should have brought popcorn to watch this show. Witnessing Ruggles crawl on the floor is highly entertaining."

"Why don't you help too?" I asked as I scanned the ground for another cricket.

He grinned. "I wouldn't want to take away the fun from all of you."

Chase crowed in victory as he caught another cricket.

"See what I mean?" Dylan asked.

Ten minutes later, Dr. Ruggles clapped his hands. "Stop! Stop! Go to your seats please. We caught all the crickets we can for now. Please return the classroom to normal."

Kids pushed their desks across the floor back to their places.

Dr. Ruggles adjusted his toupee on his head in the reflection of a metal filing cabinet in the corner of the room before facing us again. "I hope this wasn't someone's idea of a funny prank. Because if it is, I will find out who did this, and that student will be kicked out of the program."

"Why does he think it's on purpose?" I whispered to Colin.

Colin wiped his glasses on the hem of his T-shirt before setting them back on the tip of his nose. "At the start of class, he said when he got here this morning the tops of both cricket aquariums were open. My guess is they were opened last night sometime because most of the crickets had escaped into the room. Dr. Ruggles was steamed."

Dr. Ruggles pointed at us. "Discovery Camp is not playtime. You have the opportunity to learn *real* science. You were hand-selected to be part of this program. Don't fritter that away for a practical joke."

"Did he just say fritter?" I heard someone behind me whisper.

Dr. Ruggles folded his arms. "Mr. White, if I find out that one of the campers is behind this, I will hold Discovery Camp responsible."

I turned to see Dylan's reaction. The counselor paled.

Ava ninja-caught a cricket as it hopped onto her desk and then shot me a superior look. Oh great, not only did she not like me, but she had ninja skills. Just what I needed. Dr. Ruggles dusted his hands off on his lab coat. "Now, let's salvage what class time we have left, as it seems that most of the crickets have been caught and returned to their aquariums."

Chirp! Chirp!

Dr. Ruggles glared at the noise, and I covered my mouth to stop the laughter bubbling up inside.

"What did Dr. Comfrey want to talk to you about?" Colin asked as we followed Hydrogen across campus to the cafeteria for lunch.

I slowed my pace, so that the others in class wouldn't overhear. "She told me she was happy I applied for Discovery Camp."

I didn't tell Colin my science scores were higher than his. He didn't need to know that.

I kicked a pebble off of the sidewalk with the toe of my sneaker. "She said there needs to be more girls in the sciences."

"What about Ava? She's a girl too. Why didn't she pull her aside and tell her that too?"

I shrugged. "Maybe she already had." I lowered my voice. "Is Ava from out of town?"

Colin pushed his glasses up the bridge of his nose. "No, Ava lives here in Killdeer. She's in our grade too."

Terrific.

"Is anyone else in Hydrogen from Killdeer?"

"Spenser lives here too. He'll be in eighth and lives a couple of blocks from us."

That might be good. Spenser was built like a tank. Maybe if I got to know him better he could protect me from Ava's glares—or at least block my view of them.

I quickened my pace. The class was well ahead of us now. "Don't you think it's strange that both of our classes today had problems?"

"I don't know." Colin shrugged. "Camp just started. There are bound to be problems. Bergita always says 'be suspicious of a perfect day.'"

"What does that mean?"

"Beats me." His brow wrinkled. "I guess that crickets getting loose was strange."

"And the missing markers," I added.

Colin pulled on the straps hanging from his backpack. "That's not something that is really wrong. She just forgot where she put them. I mean, it's not like the crickets." He leaned closer. "I think Ruggles is right. That was deliberate."

"Remember Dr. Comfrey said that not only were the markers at the board missing, but the ones she keeps in her storage closet were gone too." I sidestepped a crack on the pavement. "If they are related, it's almost like someone is trying to sabotage the camp."

"Why would someone take her markers?"

"Why would someone let Dr. Ruggles's crickets loose?"

He frowned. "Good point. But that doesn't mean they're related."

I stopped arguing with Colin when I saw Polk painting a park bench with a fresh coat of purple paint. Michael Pike's school colors were purple and gold, and the mascot was a mountain goat. I had questioned Amelie about this mascot. She said it must be because Killdeer was in the foothills of the Appalachian Mountains. When I told her the Appalachians were too small to have mountain goats, and the closest mountain goats were in the Rockies, she said, "I got nothing."

Curie, Polk's beagle, snoozed a few feet away under an oak tree.

As our classmates passed Polk, they stepped as far away from him as they could without leaving the sidewalk. I wasn't sure if it was his paintbrush or Polk himself they avoided.

"Let's stop and talk to Polk," I said, picking up my pace.

Colin pulled on my backpack. "Why?"

It was a reasonable question. I didn't have an answer for Colin, at least not one that would make sense to his logical mind. Polk reminded me of someone who lost someone or something. His sad expression was one I saw on my sister's face sometimes when she let her guard down. It was one I saw in my own reflection when I least expected it.

I approached the elderly man without answering Colin's question. "Hi," I said to Polk.

Colin stood a little behind me and watched as our class disappeared into the cafeteria. Dylan waved them into the building but didn't seem to notice he was two kids short. If we had been in Madison's group, she would have noticed and made a note of it on her clipboard.

Polk dipped his brush into the can of purple paint. "Well, hello." This close to him I could see his eyes were more than just slits after all. They were bright blue but set so deep into his wrinkles that I didn't notice the color until the sunlight caught them.

"I'm Andi," I said.

"Hello, Andi." He nodded at Colin. "Hello, Colin."

"Hi," Colin said.

"How is Bergita? She talks about you often when I see her about town."

Colin shrugged. "Good. But she's always good. She's Bergita."

Polk chuckled and dipped his paintbrush into the paint can. "Bergita tells me that you are very bright, but you are a little young to be students here."

"We're in Discovery Camp," Colin said.

Polk braced his hand on his leg as he straightened his spine. "Very good. Do you have a favorite class at camp?"

"I like chemistry," I said.

"That was my favorite too. I was an excellent student in chemistry," he frowned and blinked rapidly. "Maybe too good," he paused. "Or too confident."

I wanted to ask him what he meant by that, but Colin pulled on my arm. "Andi, come on. Hydrogen is inside the dining hall. We've been late once already today."

"It was nice to meet you," I called over my shoulder as Colin dragged me away.

"You too, Andi Boggs," Polk said. "You too."

It wasn't until I was in line for cheese pizza I

realized I had never told him my last name. I pushed the thought aside. Bergita probably told him.

Colin selected a cheeseburger from the cafeteria line and followed me to Hydrogen's table. During lunchtime, we were supposed to eat with our element groups to "build a team atmosphere." At least that's what Madison said when she announced this rule on the first day of camp. I slid into a seat next to Chase, who was inhaling one of the four pieces of pizza on his plate, and Colin sat on my other side.

Through the window, I watched Polk and Curie strolling across the lawn. Polk held the paintbrush in one hand and the paint bucket in the other.

Ava was across the table. "What's so fascinating out the window, Andi?"

I picked up my pizza. "Nothing."

She twirled her straw in her cup. "It must be nice to have time to daydream. Some of us don't have that kind of time."

I frowned. "What are you talking about?"

Ava curled her lip. "Some of us don't have the free time to stare out the window because we have to work hard for what we have, like our places here at the camp. We didn't have it handed to us because our aunts work for the university."

I dropped my pizza back onto my plate. So that was what she was upset about. She thought I was given the spot in Discovery Camp because Amelie was Michael Pike faculty. I should have known. I didn't think it was a good idea to tell her I earned the spot with the highest test scores in science. That wouldn't make her hate me any less.

Her black eyes narrowed. "Camp is only supposed to accept the best and brightest in science. We applied months ago. You toss in your application at the last second and are accepted like that." She pointed the straw at me. "That sounds like favoritism to me."

Colin set his burger back on his plate. "How would you know when she applied?"

"I just know," Ava said.

Colin's face turned red. "Andi just moved here and didn't know about the program before the deadline. She just moved here because—Omph!"

I jabbed Colin in the side with my elbow. The last thing I wanted was for him to tell Ava about my parents' death.

Ava forked a cherry tomato on her plate. The seeds flew out, hitting Jake in the face. He blinked and then closed his eyes again. "They made an exception for her," Ava said. "They shouldn't have. She could apply for next summer."

Dylan, who had been wandering around the cafeteria during most of lunch, tugged on the back of Ava's long ponytail. "Give it a rest, Ava. There is no need to be jealous of Andi. We have enough room for two smart girls in our group."

She yanked her ponytail from his grasp. "Why would *I* be jealous of *her*?"

Good question.

At the end of the camp day, the campers poured out of Colburn. There was a small parking lot behind the science building. Most of the kids had parents waiting there, ready to drive them home.

I watched as Ava climbed into a pickup truck with a boy who was a few years older than my sister. He must have been her older brother. The brother didn't look all that excited about his role as chauffeur. I bet Bethany would have the same sullen expression on her face when she started driving and had to take me anywhere. Something to look forward to.

Colin spun the combination on his bike lock.

"Don't do that yet," I said.

He blinked at me. "Why not?"

I leaned against my bike. "Amelie is at a meeting in Columbus today and gave me some books to return to the library. I just remembered them. Let's go drop them off first."

He shrugged. "Okay."

I pulled the three literary criticisms out of my backpack. My aunt was an English professor.

"We have to be quick about it." Colin stood. "Bergita knows we should be home by four fifteen on the dot. She's not above sending out a search party if we are even two minutes late."

"Text her then."

Colin removed his cell phone from the pocket of his shorts.

Immediately after he sent the text, his phone beeped. "Bergita says be home by four forty-five." He dropped the phone back into his shorts pocket. "My parents will be home for dinner tonight, and she wants me to beat them there." There was a wistful sound in Colin's voice. His parents were doctors and rarely home. I didn't say it to Colin, but I hoped for his sake they showed up.

Colin followed me across the green. We walked around the corner of College Church. It was the church Bergita attended. I had been there a couple of times with Colin since moving to Killdeer. The door to the church creaked, and Polk stepped outside. This time he carried a stepladder. There was no sign of Curie the beagle.

I dropped to a squat around the side of the building, clutching the library books to my chest.

"What are you doing?" Colin whispered.

"Shh." I put a finger to my lips.

Colin sighed and squatted next to me.

Polk whistled, and Curie's head popped out of the bushes on the far side of the church steps. She trotted toward her master.

"I wish I could teach Jackson to come when I whistle for him," Colin muttered. "Actually, I wish I could train Jackson to do anything. He won't even play dead."

"Shh," I hissed.

Colin was quiet for half a second and then asked, "Are you going to go talk to him?"

I stood. "Yes."

Colin wiped his glasses on the hem of his T-shirt before setting them back on his nose. "Why are you so interested in him? He's just the janitor."

I ignored Colin's question and was about to step out around the side of the building when someone came around the church from the other way.

"Is that Dr. Comfrey?" Colin whispered.

I shushed him again. She wasn't wearing her lab coat, but it was the chemistry professor all right. "I thought I'd find you here," she said to Polk.

Polk reached a hand out to her, but she stepped back. His hand, still wearing the black leather glove, fell to his side.

She frowned. "You should stay away from my lab."

His face fell. "Why?"

"Items have turned up missing, and there have been other incidents too. It's safer if you stay away."

Colin whispered. "The markers? The crickets?"

"Shush!" I said.

"You think *I* took those things. You think *I* caused the incidents." He stated these as facts, not as questions.

She shook her head. "No, of course I don't, but others will."

"Like who?"

"I don't have to tell you. You already know." She took a breath. "It's not just small office supplies disappearing anymore. Some expensive equipment has gone missing. I had no choice but to tell security about the theft."

"What has gone missing?"

"The mineral scale for one. That's the most expensive item."

"Maybe you misplaced it."

She scowled. "You sound just like security. I didn't misplace a forty-pound mineral scale."

He ran his hand down the side of his face. "I should think not."

"That's not the only thing missing. Some precious metals are gone too. Copper and palladium. Only certain people would know their value."

"And you think I am one of them?"

She raised her chin. "Aren't you?"

He said nothing but dropped his gaze to the top of his shoes.

"There's another thing that has been bothering me," the chemistry professor said. "It might not be related, but ..."

"What is it?" Polk asked.

"My chemical closet was reorganized from top to bottom over the weekend. Every single powder and liquid was moved. It took me the entire day Sunday to put it back into order. What a disaster it would have been if I discovered the closet in that condition on the first day of camp."

"Why would anyone do that?"

She shook her head. "I don't know. What if I grabbed the wrong powder during an experiment? I know it's unlikely, but I am so used to finding everything right where I put it, I could have made that mistake. If I had, an experiment could have gone terribly wrong."

"Do you have any idea who did it?"

She shifted her feet. "I suspected Dylan. He's one of my top students and a counselor this week. When he was a freshman, he and some friends took all of the elements out of the closet, hid them in another part of the lab, and filled the closet with fallen leaves. They thought they were being funny. But it was a mess and almost got them all kicked out of the chemistry program. I would have never known it was them if security hadn't caught them red-handed while on their rounds." She took a breath. "I asked Dylan at length about it yesterday."

"And?"

"Nothing. If he did it or knows who did, he's not sharing." She paused. "I never reported it to security, and besides, most likely it's not related to the thefts."

"Maybe it was."

She shook her head. "No. Everything that has gone missing was there Sunday when I put the closet back together."

The wrinkles on Polk's face seemed to grow even deeper.

"Security is making extra rounds of that side of campus and especially near Colburn Hall. They will notice if anyone is in the building during off hours. You could lose your job, and if they think I helped you, I could lose mine too."

His hunched forward. "I understand. I would never want to put your job at risk. I would never want what happened to me to happen to you."

She nodded. "I appreciate that, and I am sorry. I'm really sorry."

A breeze blew across the green and over our backs. It blew my hair into my face. I brushed it away to see Curie sniffing the wind.

Sniff, sniff, went the dog's black nose, and then she turned to where Colin and I hid.

I pushed Colin back. "We have to go. Now," I said in a harsh whisper.

Curie was standing now.

"You see something, Girl?" Polk asked.

Dr. Comfrey rolled her eyes. "It's probably a squirrel."

Curie took a few steps toward us, but Polk bent down and held her back by her collar. The beagle howled like she was on the hunt and Colin and I were raccoons.

"Run," I said to Colin. We ran all the way back to our bikes. Every three strides I glanced behind me expecting to see Curie on our tails, but she never appeared.

Colin pedaled back to our neighborhood at top speed. I kept him in my sight, but I rode at a slower pace. I was too preoccupied with what we had just overheard between Dr. Comfrey and Polk.

Colin waved at me as he turned into his driveway. Bergita stood on the front porch with her hands on her hips. Jackson the pug lay at her feet. "You just made it. Your parents will be here in ten minutes. Get your keister inside and wash up. Do me a favor and put on a clean shirt too." She waved at me before she spun around and went back inside the house.

I parked my own bike inside of my garage. Amelie's car wasn't there. Her meeting in Columbus must have taken longer than she expected. It was hard to guess when my aunt would be home from work each night. I wondered if her schedule was so unpredictable because it was summer or if this was what it would be like when the school year began too. Not that it mattered. Bethany and I knew how to fend for ourselves. I could make so many different kinds of sandwiches with peanut butter that I deserved my own cooking show on the topic.

Our parents had missed dinner with us countless times because they were absorbed in their research. Because they had been so dedicated to their work, my parents found five plants in Central America that weren't known to science until they videoed, photographed, and collected samples of them.

Sometimes I'd wondered if Mom and Dad had loved Bethany and me as much as they loved their plants. I knew Bethany wondered the same thing. But neither of us would ever share this fear with the other because if we did, it might mean it was true.

I opened the front door. Bethany lay across the couch. Her long tan legs hung limply over the couch's arm. Mr. Rochester, Amelie's gentlemanly orange tabby, lay on the back of it. Mr. Rochester was a prim and proper cat, and most of the time I thought he should be wearing a bowtie. I wouldn't be the least bit surprised if he agreed with me on that point.

"How did it go at Camp Geek?" my sister asked.

I dropped my backpack by the front door. It landed with a thud. The library books I had promised Amelie I'd drop off at the library were still inside of it. "It's not called Camp Geek. How did it go at Camp Lazy?" Since moving to Killdeer, my sister hadn't shown interest in anything except a short painting class she took with Bergita at the beginning of the summer. The rest of summer break, she had lain around the house growing mold.

Bethany's eyes narrowed as she propped herself up on her elbows, and her straight blond hair fell down her back. I ran my tongue along the front of my braces. It wasn't fair that Bethany got the straight teeth *and* the straight hair.

My sister swung her legs over the arm of the couch and sat up. "It should be called Camp Geek," she said, ignoring my comeback. "That's what it is, isn't it? Only geeks need apply, right?"

Mr. Rochester jumped off the back of the couch and walked over to me. I picked him up and fell into an armchair facing the couch. "Do you wish you were in Discovery Camp too?"

She snorted. "No. Why would I want to be stuck in a classroom all day *before* school starts? Besides, I'm going into *high* school, so I'm too old for Camp Geek."

I folded my leg under me. "Stop calling it that."

Mr. Rochester found a comfortable position on my lap.

"Amelie's not home yet?" I asked even though I knew the answer.

She shook her head. "She's not any different than Mom and Dad were. I know the drill."

I frowned and scratched Mr. Rochester behind the ears.

She slid her cell phone out of her pocket. "Where's your sidekick?" she asked, meaning Colin.

"His parents will be home tonight for dinner."

A sadness flashed across my sister's face. "I hope they show up."

Just then, Amelie walked into the door. "Andi, you beat me home. I planned to be back by three, but the traffic was terrible." She laughed and pushed her long blond curls out of her eyes. Her flowered maxi dress ballooned around her long legs when she dropped her tote bag on the floor next to my backpack. My aunt pointed at the mantel. "Is that clock right? Is it really almost five? I guess we should start thinking about dinner. What do you guys want?"

Neither Bethany nor I answered, but Amelie didn't seem to notice. She perched on the arm of a chair. "While I was coming home, campus security called my cell phone. I guess they had been looking for me on campus today."

I stood up straight. "What did security want?"

Worry creased her forehead. "Apparently, things have gone missing in another building. Security told me to keep an eye out for anything suspicious and make sure the doors were locked when I left my building. They know I am usually the last person out. Of course, they will check the locks too when they make their rounds."

"He must have meant the chemistry lab. When my group got to the lab this morning, Dr. Comfrey couldn't find her dry erase markers, and—"

Bethany fell back onto the couch and howled with laughter. "Markers! They're beefing up security over markers? We did move to the sticks."

I folded my arms. "I was going to say I heard her mention that an expensive scale was taken from the lab too. She said it weighs forty pounds."

Amelie frowned. "Why would anyone steal a scale from the lab?"

"Drugs," Bethany said matter-of-factly. "They steal them for meth labs."

Amelie's mouth fell open. "How do you know that?"

"I watch the news."

Amelie stood up. "I'm sure it's nothing like that. There aren't any meth labs in Killdeer. This is a quiet town."

Bethany rolled her eyes. "Right."

"Whatever was stolen for whatever reason, we just have to keep an eye out for strange activity. That means you too, Andi, since you're there for camp."

Bethany grinned. "It would be a bummer if someone swiped a copy of the periodic table."

I rolled my eyes at Bethany.

"How does frozen pizza sound for dinner?" my aunt asked.

Bethany frowned. "We had that last night."

"Oh, that's right." Amelie fluffed her skirt and reminded me of a toddler at a tea party. "How about I call and have fresh pizza delivered?"

Bethany groaned. "I never thought I would say it, but I am over pizza." She stood. "I'm going to my room." She climbed to the stairs.

"Aren't you hungry?" Amelie asked.

"I'll make a peanut butter and jelly sandwich for myself later. Don't worry. Andi and I are used to it." She went up the stairs. Mr. Rochester jumped off my lap and followed her.

Amelie arched her brow at me. "I like pizza," was all I said.

Amelie ordered the pizza after all. She and I ate sitting at the kitchen counter. Bethany eventually showed up and ate a slice even though she was "over pizza."

After dinner, I volunteered to clean up the kitchen, which took all of two minutes since we drank our pop directly from the can and ate our pizza straight out of the box. Mrs. Cragmeyer, the fussy elderly lady who Bethany and I lived with right after our parents died, would have had a heart attack if she saw us. She thought casual meals were ones without cloth napkins.

Besides my bedroom, the kitchen was my favorite place in the house. Behind the dining table, where we never ate, there were three large picture windows that looked out onto the trees in the side yard which separated our property from the Carters'. If I stood in just the right spot, I could see through the trees and into the Carters' living room.

While throwing the pop cans into the recycling bin, I glanced out the window and saw Colin sitting on the couch. Jackson was on his lap, licking his face, including his glasses, and Bergita patted her grandson's shoulder.

I frowned. His parents didn't show. How many times had the same expression crossed my face when my parents didn't come home when they promised?

I dropped the last can into the bin and found my aunt, curled up on the couch with a book of poetry in the living room.

"Can I go over to Colin's?" I paused. "I want to talk to him about a camp project."

That was true. I did want to talk to Colin about a project, just not one assigned by a professor. Amelie didn't need to know that minor detail.

She didn't even look up from her book. "Sure. Be back when the streetlights come on."

Before running over to Colin's house, I headed upstairs. On the second floor, there was a second narrower staircase that led up into my attic bedroom. Before the staircase had been built, the attic could be reached by a folding ladder. That changed when Amelie had a nightmare about me being stuck in the attic during a fire. She called a contractor the next morning. He removed the folding hatch ladder, cut a wider hole in the hallway's ceiling, and made the narrowest set of stairs I'd ever seen. They were barely big enough for my oversized feet. Luckily the opening was near the end of the hallway, so it didn't really block anything else and the contractor made the stairs appear like they came out of the wall and had always been there.

Mr. Rochester loved the new staircase. He had never been a big fan of the ladder. Most of the time, I liked the stairs too. It was easier and faster to reach my room. The downside was every time someone went into the bathroom in the middle of the night it woke me up because the staircase was right next to the bathroom door, and I didn't have a door anymore. I had two fans running in my room all the time to block the noise.

I tiptoed up the stairs, not because I was trying to be quiet but because it was the best way to climb the narrow steps.

Mr. Rochester was already in my room lying on the lid of my closed laptop in the middle of my desk. He pawed at the middle desk drawer as if he knew exactly what I was searching for.

I eyed the cat. "How did you know that I came up here for the casebook?"

He meowed. Mr. Rochester knew everything.

I opened the drawer and removed the casebook. I flipped through the pages of Colin's and my first case. We had searched for and found a long-lost relative in my family tree. Would we be able to find out what was happening in the science building? Or how Dr. Comfrey and Polk knew each other? I hoped Bergita had some answers. She had proven to be a valuable source of town information in the past.

I tucked the casebook under my arm, patted the cat on the head, and tiptoed down the stairs. At the last step, I almost collided with Bethany as she stepped out of the bathroom. Bathroom door-staircase collisions were another hazard of the new set up.

"Watch where you're going," Bethany snapped.

"Sheesh, sorry. I didn't know you were in there."

She spotted the casebook under my arm and rolled her eyes. "Are you going to play detective again?"

"What do you care? You said you weren't interested in this stuff."

She sniffed. "Trust me. I'm not. Where's Amelie?"

"In the living room, reading."

She spun around, hitting me in the face with her hair. I knew *that* was on purpose. After waiting a second to make sure I was out of hair-whipping range, I followed her.

When Bethany and I stepped into the living room, Amelie set her book beside her on the couch. "Andi, I thought you were going to Colin's?"

"I am." I waved to them as I went out the door. On the porch, I left the door open just a millimeter, so I could hear their conversation. I put my eye to the crack. Bethany didn't usually make an effort to talk to our aunt alone. Whatever she said to Amelie, I wanted to hear it.

My sister's back was to me, and she blocked Amelie from my view. Bethany folded her arms. "Mrs. Cragmeyer called me today. She said she would love to have me come stay with them, so I could go to school with my friends."

I swallowed hard. The Cragmeyers were a stuffy older couple who used to watch us when our parents were off in a jungle somewhere hunting for plants. After our parents died in January, Amelie made arrangements with the Cragmeyers for us to live with them the remainder of the school year, so that we wouldn't have to change schools midyear. Mrs. Cragmeyer didn't care for me. My hair was too curly. I was too awkward and too bookish for her. Beautiful Bethany was another story, but my sister didn't care about Mrs. Cragmeyer any more than I did. It was the idea of starting high school back home with her friends that made Bethany ask.

Amelie sighed. "Mrs. Cragmeyer shouldn't have made an offer like that without checking with me first. Besides, we talked about this before. You are staying here in Killdeer with Andi and me. That's final."

"Why? That's not fair. I don't want to be here. Mrs. Cragmeyer understands that. She cares about me and knows I will be happier with my friends."

Another sigh from my aunt. "I'm glad she cares about you, I really am, but that doesn't change the fact I am your guardian and—"

"I have the right to decide where I'll live and where I'll go to school."

"Actually, you don't." There was an unfamiliar edge in Amelie's voice. "You're only fourteen years old."

"I'll be eighteen in four years."

"Then we will talk about this again when you're eighteen."

"You won't get my parents' money if I move. Is that the problem?"

There was silence. Then my aunt said, "I'm going to ignore that comment because I know you're upset."

"That only means it's true."

"Bethany, I know it's been a difficult move for you. And I know it's hard for you to be away from

53

everything and everyone you know, but hating it so much is not going to change your circumstances. Look at Andi, she seems to be doing so well."

I winced. Comparing Bethany to me was *not* the way to go.

"I'm so glad that Andi is thriving in the middle of nowhere." Bethany shook as she spoke. "That's because there is a super nerd right next door just like her. Who have I met since I moved here besides Bergita? Is she going to hang out with me in the cafeteria? I don't think so."

"That will change when school starts. You will make new friends."

"I don't *want* new friends." Bethany's voice broke. "I want *my* friends."

"Your parents asked me to care for you and Andi. That means making the decisions that I think are in your best interest. I don't think living with the Cragmeyers is the best thing for you." She paused. "If you want a friend to visit from your old school before the school year starts, that's fine with me."

"Why would one of my friends come out here? There's nothing to do here."

"They might like visiting the country. Maybe I can meet their mom or dad halfway. How does that sound?"

"It's not the same as living there."

"It's not, but it's something and all I have to offer you. Take it or leave it."

I felt something wet on the back of my leg, and I covered my mouth with my hand to stifle a scream.

Jackson, Colin's pug, licked my bare calf.

"Shoo! Jackson," I hissed as I peered back through the crack in the door, but by then Bethany had left the room and my aunt was back to reading her poetry.

Colin watched me from the front yard. "Why are you spying on your house?"

I put a finger to my lips. Quietly, I closed the door the rest of the way with a light click and followed Jackson down the porch steps.

When we were safely on the lawn, I shook my finger at the pug. "You almost gave me away, Mister."

Jackson's tongue hung out of his mouth as he gave me a doggy grin. Bergita scolded him so much I doubted he even noticed anymore.

I noticed the leash hanging from the pug's collar. "Are you walking Jackson?" I'd tried to walk the pug once. We made it to the driveway before Jackson wanted to go home.

Colin nodded. "He needs to burn off some of the snacks he eats."

Jackson's grin disappeared. He wasn't much for exercise. He preferred to sleep on his pillow.

"How was dinner with your parents?" I hoped I had been wrong about his parents' not showing up for dinner.

Colin leaned over to pick up Jackson's leash. "They couldn't get away from the hospital. There was an accident on the highway, and they had to stay there and help out."

"That's scary." I examined the cover of the casebook. Ever since my parents' death, "accident" had taken on a new meaning.

"Dad said that it wasn't a bad accident, or at least that's what Bergita told me he said in his text to her."

"I'm sorry. I know you wanted to see them."

He shrugged and wrapped Jackson's leash tightly around his hand. "They save people's lives. Having dinner with me isn't going to do any good like that."

It might, I thought. I wished my parents had been home more. I wished I had thought to ask them to stay home. They saved lives too by finding exotic plants that had the potential to cure diseases someday. But the plants didn't save my parents or the time Bethany and I missed out with them. I didn't say any of this to Colin. Maybe someday I would be brave enough to tell him.

"Is that the casebook?" Colin asked.

"Yep. We need to talk about opening a new case."

Colin's face lit up. "Really? You mean Boggs and Carter Investigations is back in action?"

I grinned. "It's clear we need to find out what's going on at Discovery Camp. It's more than missing markers. Questioning Bergita is a good place to start."

"Let's go." Colin ran toward his house only to be jerked backward by Jackson. Jackson didn't move that fast for anyone. "Sorry, Jacks." He scooped up the pug, and we both ran across the yard.

The front door slammed after us when we went inside the Carters' house. Bergita came in from the kitchen, wiping her hands on a towel. "Back so soon?"

"Jackson's heart wasn't into the walk," Colin set the dog on the carpet.

The little dog waddled over to Bergita and sniffed at her hand with the hopes of a treat.

"Always thinking with your stomach, aren't you?" Colin's grandmother tsked, shaking her finger at the dog. She wore her silver hair in a high ponytail on the top of her head and looked more like a cheerleader than a grandma.

She smiled at me. "Andi, you're just in time for dessert. I made pineapple upside-down cake. It will rot your teeth, but it's worth it."

I reminded myself to floss when I got home.

Bergita stepped through the archway that led into the kitchen. Jackson hurried after her. She peered down at him over her hot pink reading glasses. "Oh, you want some too, do you, old pork chop?"

Jackson didn't seem to mind the nickname as he waited expectantly at the end of the island.

My mouth fell open. The largest pineapple

upside-down cake I had ever seen sat in the middle of the island. It was three tiers high. "Bergita, you weren't kidding when you said the cake would rot our teeth. If we eat all of that, our teeth will fall out."

Bergita snorted. "Now, you hush. I tried a new recipe. It wasn't until about halfway through mixing the batter that I realized I was following the measurements for a wedding cake. My only option was to keep going or I would waste all that precious batter. And besides, Colin's father loved pineapple upside-down cake as a child. He could eat half of it in one sitting."

Colin was slack-jawed as he stared at the cake. "Mom and Dad won't eat it." He glanced at me. "They don't touch refined sugar. They are both health nuts and hit the gym at the hospital every day before their shifts."

Bergita's eyes twinkled. "Your mother might not, but mark my words, your father has a secret sweet tooth. I bet a piece goes missing in the middle of the night. Just between the four of us," she nodded at Jackson to let him know he was included, "I may have made the cake this large to irritate your mother. I hoped she would turn that particular shade of purple she does when she thinks I am trying to pull her chain. It's fun."

I laughed.

"Bergita," Colin said with a sigh.

"Ahh, it'll give your parents reason to daydream about putting me in an old folks' home. Little do they know, I plan to live well into the triple digits. I'll show them." She gave a curt nod.

"I don't think it's a good idea to make Dad mad."

"If I can't tease my own son and daughter-in-law from time to time, what do I have?"

Jackson put his paws on one of the dining chairs.

She wagged her finger at him. "No cake for you. Sugar isn't good for dogs, but I have something you'll like."

"Bergita, I think you might be the reason Jackson is so chubby," I said with a laugh.

She removed a piece of beef jerky from a plastic jar on the kitchen counter. "Oh, the vet is going to lecture me about his weight during his next appointment." She sighed. "But how can I say no to that face?"

Jackson grabbed the jerky and shimmied under the china cabinet. It was a tight fit, but he made it.

She clapped her hands. "Now, both of you take a seat at the table and I will cut you a slice."

Colin and I fell into the chairs around the oak dining table. There were still places set for Colin's parents.

The piece of cake Bergita put in front of me was enormous. I took a bite and my teeth ached. The yellow cake melted in my mouth, and the pineapple was so sweet. I wiped whipped cream from my upper lip.

"Yum," Colin said with his mouth full of cake.

Bergita smiled. "So how was camp today? You kids get any smarter? The summer I was twelve, I learned to skip stones down on the reservoir, not how to build a rocket ship or whatever it is you're doing."

"We aren't building rockets," I said to Bergita, and then Colin and I shared a look.

Bergita set her mug of tea on the table. "Why do I have the same feeling I get when Jackson wiggles under the sofa after knocking a glass off the coffee table? What are you two up to?"

"We aren't up to anything," Colin said.

Bergita pursed her lips. "You shouldn't lie to your grandmother. I'm old and could keel over at any moment. What if the last thing you told me was a lie, then how would you feel?"

"You just said that you planned to live into your triple digits to torment Mom and Dad."

She grinned. "Well, I suppose I did."

"Honest," I said. "We aren't up to anything."

"I'm always suspicious when kids say 'honest.' It makes me think the opposite. If you were really honest, would you have to profess that? Hmmm?" She looked from Colin to me and back again.

I licked my forked. "We aren't up to anything, but someone at Michael Pike is."

Bergita cut herself a big slice of cake, twice the size of mine.

I gasped at the piece.

She snorted. "I'm over seventy. If I can double up on my carbs, I'm going to do it."

Colin rolled his eyes.

She forked a piece of cake. "So tell me what this someone else has been up to."

"Stealing," I said. "At least, that's what we think. Things have gone missing from the chemistry lab recently. They may have been stolen."

She ran her fork through the whipped cream. "What types of things?"

"Markers—"

"Wait, did you say markers? Who cares about markers? I'll buy the chemistry lab a carton if they are so hard up for markers."

"That's not all. An expensive scale is missing too."

"Hmm," Bergita said. "Is that your casebook?" Bergita pointed to the notebook beside my place at the table. "Does this mean you two plan to investigate these lab supply disappearances?"

I nodded. My mouth was too full of cake to speak.

"We want to solve the mystery," Colin said.

I swallowed. "How do you know Polk?"

She held her mug. "Polk? He's from Killdeer. I know he's from around town. You live here long enough you meet everyone. Maybe not the college kids that come and go, but everyone else." She squinted at me. "What does Polk have to do with this?"

I lowered my voice. "A lot. I think he's at the center of the whole thing."

Bergita stabbed her cake. "That's what I was afraid you'd say."

"Why do you say that, Bergita?" I asked.

Bergita stirred another scoop of sugar into her tea. "Because Polk is the sort of man who is blamed for things gone wrong whether he did them or not. Why do you think Polk is involved?"

"He hangs around Colburn, the science building, a lot." I shot a glance at Colin. "And we saw him talking to our chemistry professor. It was odd."

"Odd? Why? Polk is a janitor there. Maybe he was asking her if she needed a lightbulb replaced."

I shrugged. "When they spoke, Dr. Comfrey told Polk to stay away from the building."

Colin pushed up his glasses with the handle end of his fork. "She thought security might think he did it because of the things that went missing."

"The markers," Bergita said. "Does Polk like to draw?"

I frowned. "We already said that it's more than markers. A scale is missing and some precious metals, copper and ..." I trailed off.

"Palladium," Colin jumped in. "She said the palladium was missing too, and only certain people would know its worth. Polk was one of them."

"How would he know?" Bergita set down her fork.

"We were hoping you could tell us," I said.

"Maybe you should talk to Amelie about this. She must know your chemistry professor better than I do since she works there. And I have no idea why Polk would take those items from the lab."

"What *do* you know about him?" Colin asked.

She peered into her tea. "He's harmless, and he's a tortured soul."

Colin's brow wrinkled. "A tortured soul? What does that mean?"

Bergita sighed. "Polk has had a sad life."

"Why's that?" Colin asked through a mouthful of cake.

"Can you swallow before you ask a question? Goodness, your mother will think I raised you in a barn."

Colin took a swig of milk. "Why do you say he's had a sad life?"

"Because it is true." She stirred her tea. This time it was a Mickey Mouse mug. Bergita was partial to cartoon characters when it came to her dishes. I wondered if this was another trait she adopted to annoy her son and daughter-in-law. She blew on the hot liquid. "I don't know the particulars, but something must have happened to him to give him that constant hangdog expression. He doesn't look much different in the face from his beagle."

Now that she mentioned it, Polk did resemble Curie a little.

"Did you ever ask him what was wrong?" I asked.

She shook her head. "I figured he would tell me if he wanted to. I wouldn't say that we were particularly close, but we were neighborly, just like everyone in Killdeer is. But you rarely learn the deep dark secrets about your neighbors. That's probably for the best. We have conversations is all. We chat when I see him out and about, but that doesn't happen as often as it used to. He's getting up there in age. I wouldn't be surprised if he was pushing eighty."

Colin took a big gulp of milk before he spoke. He swallowed. "Do you think Polk would steal from the chemistry lab?"

"My first thought would be 'no,' but I can't say for sure. If a person is desperate enough, they will do some crazy things."

"What kind of things?" I asked.

She shook her head as if she didn't want to discuss it.

Colin eyed my half-eaten piece of cake. I pushed the plate toward him without a word. "Where does he live?" Colin asked.

She frowned. "I don't know. I guess somewhere close to campus. There are a lot of apartment buildings and small houses for rent on that side of town for the university students." Her brow knit together as if she were disappointed in herself for not knowing the answer to Colin's question. "The bottom line is I know very little about Polk, other than he's a janitor at Michael Pike and has been for decades. I wish I could tell you more." She squinted at me. "I recognize that sparkle in your eye, Andi. You want to get to the bottom of this, don't you? I won't tell you not to because I know it won't do any good. Just remember, Polk has had some hard times. Don't push him too far."

I wanted to ask Bergita what she meant by not pushing Polk. What would happen if we pushed him too far? And push him where?

But before I could ask any of the dozens of questions buzzing through my head, the back door opened and the Drs. Carter stepped into the kitchen. Both of them looked tired from an extra-long shift at the hospital. I stole a glance at Colin. His face brightened with the arrival of his parents, and he jumped out of his chair.

Colin's father nodded at me. "Nice to see you, Andi." He turned to Bergita, "Mom, we're headed straight to bed. We both have early rounds." He clapped Colin on the shoulder.

I blinked. I hadn't noticed until they stood side by side how much Colin resembled his father, who was a handsome man in a studious sort of way. They had the same floppy brown hair, and the top of Colin's head was level with his father's nose. Hadn't he been shorter at the beginning of the summer? I examined my cake plate.

"But I made upside-down pineapple cake. It's your favorite." Bergita stood and made a motion to cut them each a colossal piece of cake.

Colin's father frowned and dropped his hand from

his son's shoulder. "You know we don't eat refined sugars."

Bergita set the knife on the table.

Colin's mother said with a yawn. "Like Nate said, we both have early shifts tomorrow and then meetings into the evening. We might not even cross paths at all tomorrow." She patted her son on his head as she followed her husband out of the room.

Colin watched them go.

I jumped out of my chair. "I'd better go home. The streetlights are on and Amelie is going to come looking for me." I said goodnight to Bergita and Colin and left through the back door, taking the casebook with me. Colin didn't even notice. His eyes were fixed on the doorway where his parents had disappeared, and I couldn't stop thinking that Colin must be taller than I was now. For some weird reason, that bothered me.

It wasn't until I changed into my pajamas for the night that I remembered the little piece of plastic I found in Colburn's hallway. I set it in the middle of my desk. Mr. Rochester and I stared at it until we couldn't keep our eyes open.

The next morning, I was in the kitchen eating Cheerios straight from the box, and Amelie was blinking at her iPad when Bethany flew into the room. "She's coming!"

I dropped the box of Cheerios on the counter and o's scattered over the granite surface.

"Who's coming?" Amelie replaced the cover on her iPad.

"Kaylee!" she squealed. "I called her last night after you said that I could invite a friend over from back home. Her mom just said that she can come. They are meeting us at the mall in Canton today."

Kaylee Vee was Bethany's best friend. She'd lived down the street from us most of our lives, and she and Bethany had been inseparable since kindergarten.

Amelie folded her hands on the countertop. "Today?

Bethany, I have meetings on campus all day. I can't leave work early to pick up your friend. Canton is over an hour away."

Bethany's shoulders bent forward and the excitement drained from her face. "But you said I could have a friend over."

Amelie licked her lips. "I know, but ..."

I cleaned up the Cheerios from the counter. "I'd like to see Kaylee too," I whispered.

Amelie turned to me.

I arched my eyebrows at her. *Come on, Amelie, Bethany is happy, just go with it.*

Amelie sighed. "Let me see what I can do. I can ask a colleague to cover for me, and maybe we can hang around the mall for a while and do some shopping. You can pick out a couple of things for back to school."

"Really?" Bethany beamed. I hadn't seen her this happy since the last Christmas with our parents.

Amelie's broad mouth widened into a smile. "Yes." She glanced at me. "What about you, Andi? Do you want to come with us too?"

"I can't," I said. "I have Discovery Camp. I'll stay at Colin's after camp until you guys get home. Bergita won't mind."

"You're probably right, but I will give Bergita a call anyway."

Bethany danced in place. "I'm going to call Kaylee back now!" She grabbed a granola bar off of the counter and ran out of the room.

Later that morning as Colin and I rode our bikes up the sidewalk toward Colburn Hall, a security guard in a golf cart zoomed by, swerving from the sidewalk onto the grass to avoid hitting us.

Colin hit the brakes and dropped his feet from his bicycle pedals. "Whoa!"

"Maybe someone stole a library book," I said, thinking of my aunt's books, which I still needed to return to the library, inside my backpack.

Colin laughed.

"Come on." I pedaled after the golf cart. "We have a few minutes before camp starts. I need to drop off those books, and we might just find out where the security guard was headed."

Colin followed me without arguing.

Unfortunately, I lost sight of the guard after less than a minute. I was about to head to the library when I spied Curie's tail sticking out from around the corner of the dining hall. There was a narrow sidewalk between the dining hall and library.

I slowed and hopped off my bike, walking it through the narrow spot. Colin did the same a few feet behind me. We propped our bikes on the building's stone wall.

Curie stuck her head around the corner of the dining hall. Her tail wagged a greeting before she returned her attention to whatever was around the corner.

I examined the two men at the far side of the building. "A security guard is talking to Polk."

"Can you hear what they're saying?" Colin whispered.

I shook my head. "Their voices are too low, and I'm too far away. I need to get over there."

Colin pulled on the back of my T-shirt. "You can't do that. They'll see you."

I smoothed my T-shirt. "No, they won't. See that dumpster over there?" I pointed to an enormous blue dumpster ten feet behind the two men. "I'll run to it and hide behind it. Then I'll be close enough to hear what they are saying. You stay here as the lookout."

"Okay," Colin sighed. "But that dumpster is going to stink." He brushed his bangs off his glasses. "Just hurry up. We can't be late for a second day in a row."

"I'll be fast," I promised.

The security guard's back was to me. He shook his meaty finger at Polk. The older man was half the guard's size, but he wasn't any less angry and pointed right back at the guard as he spoke. The two were so involved in the conversation I could have tap danced right by them and they wouldn't have noticed me.

Without a backward glance at Curie and Colin, I dashed across the small parking lot behind the cafeteria and dove behind the dumpster. My elbow banged on the side of the dumpster. I clapped one hand over my mouth and the other over the sore spot on my arm. There was a small gash on my forearm, but it wasn't bleeding that badly. Hopefully I wouldn't need a tetanus shot.

"So, you're telling me," the security guard said between snaps of bubble gum, "you had nothing to do with the theft at Colburn last night."

"Yes, Kip. That is what I am telling you. I left campus at seven and didn't see anything strange." Polk spoke slowly as if the security guard would understand better if he slowed his speech.

"We have you on camera going in and out of the

building on other nights. Do you deny you've been inside the building long after hours."

"No," Polk said in a low gravelly voice. "But I wasn't there last night. I'm sure your video camera tape will show that."

He folded his arms. "Last night, the camera malfunctioned, or someone made it malfunction. What would you know about that?"

Polk held onto his side as if it helped him stand upright and didn't reply.

Kip scowled. "What has sparked your sudden interest in Colburn?"

"What sudden interest? I've always checked in on that building. I work for maintenance. It's my job."

"Oh, I know that," Kip said with a nod.

I glanced back at Colin. He was waving one arm wildly and holding his nose with the other.

What was going on? Was he having some kind of fit?

Colin pointed at the ground.

I looked around my feet and saw nothing. I rolled my eyes and turned back to the two arguing men.

Kip loomed over Polk. "If you are behind these incidents I will find out."

A warm, furry body brushed against my leg. Had Curie come over to sit with me?

I scooted away from the dumpster to see if Curie was there. It was an animal all right, but it wasn't the beagle. A small skunk wiggled out from under the dumpster. I froze. Now I knew what Colin was trying to tell me. Slowly, I turned my head to Colin. He was waving at me frantically to run over to him. I shook my head and the skunk toddled a few inches away, stopping to sniff the dumpster. The skunk seemed friendly for the moment. But I was afraid if I made a break for Colin, he would turn his tail on me, and that would be bad, very bad.

Kip and Polk continued to argue a few feet away. As Kip told Polk to stay away from the science building, I noticed the janitor's eyes were focused on a spot behind me.

I looked back to the corner of the building where Colin and Curie were, just in time to see a lock of brown hair disappear around the corner. He saw Colin. I knew it.

The skunk waddled a few more steps away.

"Please leave," I breathed. "Please."

Kip grimaced. "What were you doing in Colburn after hours?"

"What do you think I was doing? I fixed stuff. It's my job."

"What stuff?"

"Anything that was broken. I don't keep a list of everything I do throughout the day in my pocket."

"What did you take from Colburn last night?" the guard's voice was friendlier than before.

Polk wasn't fooled by the other man's trick question. "Nothing! Why would I take anything? And I've already told you *three* times that I wasn't in that building last night."

"Was anyone inside the chemistry lab when you went inside there?"

"I was never there," Polk said through gritted teeth.

74

"What need would I have for anything from a chemistry lab?"

"If you didn't take it, how do you know about it?"

Polk's face dissolved. "I don't."

The skunk moved a few more paces. Maybe I would be okay. Maybe the skunk would be happy with waddling about near the dumpster. That was fine with me as long as it didn't point its behind in my direction.

Kip said something under his breath I didn't catch.

"I. Wasn't. There." Polk dug his fingers into the sleeves of his shirt. He was still wearing the gloves. I had yet to see him without his gloves on. He had to be hot in that outfit. It was the end of summer, and the temperature was already eighty degrees and climbing. I was warm in my shorts and camp T-shirt.

I inched closer to them, still in a crouched position along the side of the dumpster. When I moved, the skunk looked at me. I froze again.

Polk stepped back from the security guard and braced his hands on his upper thighs for support. "You're not going to put this on me."

Kip scowled. "I know your history."

Polk wobbled back and forth as if Kip had pushed him. "Your fa—"

"Don't even say it. You have no idea what I went through because of you."

Polk's wrinkles appeared deeper. "Not because of me."

"Yes, because of you, and—" The radio at Kip's hip crackled. He ripped it from his belt. "This is Kip."

He listened to the crackling and garbled words for a moment. "Ten four. I will be there in three." He strapped the radio back onto his belt. "You had better not be lying to me."

Polk said nothing.

The security guard marched to his golf cart and climbed in. My heart was in my throat as he started it up. If he came my way he would see Colin or me. Even worse, he might scare the skunk.

Kip revved the engine. I let out a breath when he made a tight turn and went the opposite direction from our hiding places. The skunk ran away at the noise. Thankfully, it didn't spray as it went.

Polk gave a low whistle and Curie trotted over to him. "You kids can come out now," Polk said. "The guard is gone."

I shot a worried look back to Colin. He held up his arms and shrugged. "What do we do?" he mouthed.

That was a good question. I wished I knew the answer.

"Andi, you can come out too," Polk said in his gravelly voice.

He had seen Colin, and he'd seen me too. So much for my clean run to the dumpster. Before I moved, I scanned the area to make double sure the skunk was gone.

I glanced back at where Colin was, but I couldn't see him anymore around the corner of the dining hall.

"I know you are there. I saw both of you," Polk said.

Colin's head popped out around the building. "How did you see us?"

Polk frowned. "How could I miss you with you waving your arms about like a maniac."

"There was a skunk by Andi."

Thanks for giving me away, Colin.

"That would do it. If I saw a skunk, I'd be flailing too. Now, Andi, you come on out."

I sighed and popped out from behind the dumpster.

Polk stood straighter. "Were you two spying on us?"

"Umm ..." Colin said.

I winced.

Polk watched us with the same interest with which he had examined the parched grass yesterday morning.

"How do you know Dr. Comfrey?" Colin blurted out.

I wanted to smack Colin on the backside of his head. Polk didn't know we'd spied on him and Dr. Comfrey yesterday too, and he didn't need to know that we had.

Polk didn't seem surprised by the question though. "Meg is a professor here at the college."

"Meg?" Colin asked.

He smiled and showed off two missing lower teeth. "Dr. Comfrey to you." He frowned. "You two should hurry, you will be late for camp."

Curie sat at her master's feet.

I stuck my hand into my shorts pocket and removed the piece of plastic that I found the day before. I thrust it at Polk. "What's this?"

The older man peered down at my hand. "Looks to me like a piece of plastic."

Colin's forehead creased. It was the first he had heard about the plastic.

"I know that," I said. "But what is it from? Yesterday, I thought I was in the hallway alone on the third floor of Colburn until I heard someone drop something and run away. I think this was a part of whatever was dropped."

He picked it up with his gloved fingertips. "I know what this is."

"What?" Colin and I asked at the same time.

"It's part of a mineral scale. This is the plastic slide that moves back and forth to balance the weight."

Colin gasped. "Like the scale that was stolen."

Polk nodded. "Exactly." He dropped the piece back into my open palm. "You most likely heard the person who took the scale."

"It wasn't you," I said.

He shook his head, "No. It wasn't, but why do you think I am innocent?"

"Because you couldn't have run away that quickly. I would have caught you."

This brought a smile to Polk's face. "You're right. Now, you should both go on to class."

"He's right, Andi." Colin pulled on my arm.

I shook him off. "If you didn't take the scale, why does the security guard think you did?"

The older man frowned. "You will know soon enough. Now, go on. They will wonder where you are."

Colin finally pulled me away from Polk and Curie. We raced back to our bikes. We didn't say a word as we pedaled to the science building.

The building's front door slammed behind us as we ran for the stairwell.

"Andi, we completely missed the opening and are late for chemistry," Colin hissed as we climbed the stairs to the third floor. "Bergita will ground me for a week if she finds out we skipped camp."

I frowned at him. "We didn't skip. We're just a little late."

Colin ran his hand through his hair. "Why didn't you tell me about that piece of plastic?" There was hurt in his voice.

I pushed open the heavy metal door onto the second floor and turned to look at him. "I forgot about it yesterday until after I left your house, and then I was reminded of it again when we saw Polk."

"If we are a team, we can't keep secrets."

"I'm not," I said, feeling a blush on my cheeks. "I forgot, honest."

Colin walked by me into the hall and grinned. "Oh, okay. Let's go. If we're kicked out of camp, it will go on our permanent record."

I hurried after him, relieved he was no longer angry. "Permanent record? What permanent record?"

Our footfalls echoed in the quiet hallway. The only doorway open was the chemistry lab in the middle of the hall. All the other classrooms were closed for the summer. I tried to imagine how busy the hallways must be during the school year when students and professors rushed back and forth to class.

Colin's shoes squeaked as we moved down the hall.

"If we are going to keep investigating, you'd better wear less noisy shoes tomorrow," I whispered. "How can we sneak around when everyone can hear you coming a mile away?"

Colin frowned at his shoes. "They're my new ones for school. Bergita wanted me to break them in."

I shook my head.

Two doors led into the lab. Through the first door, we heard Dr. Comfrey say, "Today, we will talk about the glucose, or simple sugar, in your favorite drinks.

Using the Bunsen burner and Benedict's solution, a combination of sodium citrate, sodium carbonate, and copper sulfate."

In silent agreement, Colin and I tiptoed past the first door and slipped through the classroom's back door into our seats.

Dr. Comfrey arched her eyebrows at us but, thankfully, didn't say anything. The professor cleared her throat. "Everyone, please put your safety goggles on." She stared pointedly at Colin and me. I glanced around the room. Everyone already wore safety goggles, including Dr. Comfrey, who was at the front lab table near her desk. On the countertop, she had a Bunsen burner, a can of cola, a bottle of apple juice, a bottled sports drink, a small blue bottle, and a row of test tubes.

Colin shoved goggles into my hand, and I slid them onto my face.

Dr. Comfrey selected one of the test tubes from the rack and poured a small amount of apple juice into it. "Apple juice first," she said, looking at us over her safety glasses. "Then we add two drops of the solution." She filled the dropper from the blue bottle, and added two drops of the liquid to the apple juice. "Final step, heating it over the flame."

I wished I'd sat closer to the front of the room for a better view of the experiment.

"Ava," Dr. Comfrey said. "Please stay in your seat. Everyone will have time for a closer look in a moment."

Ava was halfway off of her stool. I guessed I wasn't the only one wishing for a better view of the reaction.

She waited for Ava to return to her seat before she turned on the Bunsen burner's gas.

Dr. Comfrey smiled. "Here we go." The professor picked up the metal striker. A flame caught on the burner. As she moved the test tube over the flame, the burner exploded, and the classroom erupted into screams.

Flames ran up the sleeve of Dr. Comfrey's lab coat and across the papers on the lab table. The fire alarm went off. Kids covered their ears and watched in horror as Dr. Comfrey tried to muffle the fire on her left arm with her right hand.

The gas for the Bunsen burner was still on and the flame grew bigger. Dylan ran to the front of the room and shut off the gas. "Outside! Get outside!" Dylan shouted and ripped the fire extinguisher off the wall.

Kids ran from the room. Colin pulled on my sleeve. "Andi! Come on!"

Dylan sprayed Dr. Comfrey with the extinguisher. White foam covered the professor and lab table. Tears ran down the teacher's face as she slid to the floor.

The fire alarm wailed, and out in the hall, red emergency lights pulsed.

Dylan squatted down beside her. He removed his cell phone from his pocket. "Yes, I'm at Michael Pike University. There's been a fire in the chemistry lab." Dylan caught me staring. "Andi! Go outside."

I turned and ran. In the stairwell, I nearly collided with Kip, the security guard. "What are you doing in the building? Didn't you hear the fire alarm? Get outside." He didn't wait to see if I followed his orders as he took the steps two at a time to the second floor. I lingered in the stairwell for a few minutes trying to see if I could hear anything upstairs above the scream of the fire alarm. But it was no good. I ran down to the lobby and out the door.

Outside, two fire trucks and an ambulance already sat on the grass next to the science building. Dr. Ruggles and Dr. Lime, the ecology professor, stood near the truck speaking with the fire chief. Three other firemen had their masks down over their faces and marched into the building. The EMTs removed a stretcher from the back of the ambulance.

"Andi, what were you doing still inside?" Susan asked me. "Go over there with the others under the tree."

As I was about to join my classmates, I heard Madison ask, "Where's Dylan?"

"He's with Dr. Comfrey," I said. "He put out the fire."

Madison swallowed and looked away from me.

"Is Dr. Comfrey hurt?" Luis asked.

I nodded.

"Go sit with the other kids," Madison ordered.

I wanted to ask her what was going to happen to camp, but her glare gave me second thoughts.

The campers from all element groups gathered

beneath a huge oak tree. I fell onto the grass next to Colin, scanning the grounds for any sign of Polk.

"Who are you looking for?" Colin asked under his breath.

"Polk."

Colin pushed his bangs out of his eyes. "You don't think Polk—"

I shifted into a more comfortable spot on the ground. "No. Of course not."

Dylan came out of the building. There was soot on his T-shirt, and his hair stuck up in every direction.

Madison ran over to him. He held up his hand to stop her before she could touch him. I wished I could hear what they were saying. Dr. Ruggles marched over to the two college students.

"What happened?" a kid from Helium asked. Gavin and Spenser began talking at the same time.

"Boom!" Spenser bellowed. "Fire and glass everywhere. We had to dive under our desks to avoid being burnt alive."

Gavin nodded. "It was heavy stuff. We could have been killed. Or at least barbequed," he added wistfully.

"The flames were huge. Dr. Comfrey was on fire," Spenser said.

The other campers fell silent.

Ava, who leaned against the oak tree, snorted. "Please, Spenser. You're making most of that up. There was a small explosion and Dr. Comfrey's lab coat caught on fire." Her dark eyes flicked in my direction. "It seems highly suspicious to me that the lab was going fine until Andi and Colin showed up *late*. When they walked into lab, the Bunsen burner blew up."

Colin opened and closed his mouth like a goldfish.

I stood and folded my arms. "What are you trying to say, Ava?"

She shrugged. "I'm just telling the others the chain of events. Chain of events is important in the sciences, you know. I particularly find them interesting."

The other campers watched Ava and me. I could feel the blush creep up my neck, across my face, and into my hairline. I stomped to a neighboring oak tree about ten yards away and sat at the base, facing away from the other students.

Behind me I heard the other kids laughing.

Colin dashed across the yard and fell into a spot next to me. "Are you okay?"

I frowned. "I'll be okay. I just wish Ava would leave me alone. Doesn't she care that Dr. Comfrey might be seriously hurt?"

Colin's brow wrinkled. "I've known Ava since first grade. I've never seen her act like this before. Something about you gets on her nerves."

Was that supposed to make me feel better?

The door to the science building opened. It was Dr. Comfrey on a stretcher. Two firemen carefully lifted the stretcher down the three steps to the sidewalk. There was a piece of gauze, which had bled through, on the professor's face.

I stood up.

"Andi, where are you going?"

"I have to get closer," I whispered and inched toward a trash can that was halfway between Colin and the professors.

Dr. Ruggles stomped over to the chemistry professor

and Dr. Lime hurried after him, followed by Dylan. "Meg, what happened?"

The chemistry professor groaned. "I don't know. We were just doing the glucose experiment. I've done it a thousand times. The Bunsen burner just blew up."

Dr. Ruggles brushed spittle from his lip with the back of his hand. "Did you check the burner?"

She touched her left arm and then winced. "Of course, I did. The hose was fine."

Dr. Ruggles frowned. "Do you have any idea what implications this has for Discovery Camp? Not to mention the School of Sciences. What am I supposed to tell the dean?" He dropped his hand to his side. "We'll have to call the children's parents and cancel camp for the rest of the day."

"But—" Dylan began to protest.

"Don't argue with me, Mr. White. This is a serious matter. If one of the children had been injured, do you realize what a disaster that would be for the university? The thought of a wrongful death lawsuit ties my colon up in a knot."

"No one died," Dr. Comfrey said through gritted teeth.

The older professor ignored her. "We will have to receive the university's approval to reopen camp tomorrow and to keep the program going as planned."

"Not all of their parents will be able to pick them up early," Dylan said.

"Then you and other counselors will think of something to entertain them until their parents do arrive that does not involve explosions, understood?"

"Yes, sir," Dylan said.

Dr. Comfrey closed her eyes. "I suppose you're right. Their parents should be told and going back into Colburn is out of the question for the rest of the day." She opened her eyes again. "Kip says the building will be closed for the rest of the day as it is. They have to determine what caused the accident." She scowled as she said the head security guard's name.

"Ma'am," said one of the medics holding the stretcher. "This isn't a good time for talking. We have to take you to the hospital about those burns."

"Yes, I apologize," said Dr. Ruggles, straightening up. "Dr. Comfrey, go with the medics to the hospital and get stitched up. I'll take care of everything here. Unfortunately, I'm used to cleaning up other people's messes."

Dr. Comfrey touched her bloody bandage on her cheek and bit her lip as the stretcher rocked along the bumpy sidewalk to the ambulance.

Dr. Ruggles gathered the camp counselors into a small pack. "Camp is over for the day," he said. "Call the parents of each of your students. I'm going back inside to talk to Kip and the fire chief. Hopefully, I will have something sufficient to report to the university about how this happened."

I ran back to Colin and pulled him back to the rest of the class under the oak tree as the counselors joined the students.

"Hi, kiddos," Susan said, giving us a huge smile. She practically hopped in place. I could see her running back and forth on the basketball court and never breaking a sweat. "Because of the little incident in the chemistry lab, we'll be outside for a bit. That's not so bad, is it? It's a great day. Anyone want to play tag?"

"Does she think we are five?" a boy whispered to his lab partner.

Madison held her clipboard close to her chest. "We're not going to play tag." She glowered at Susan. "We need to call all of your parents to tell them what happened and assure them that you are safe."

"Are we going to have to go home?" a boy from Luis's group asked.

"That will be up to your parents. Colburn is off limits. Anyone caught inside there will be kicked out of camp," Madison said, her voice firm.

Did that just mean if you go inside but don't get caught?

Colin bit his lip. He knew what I was thinking.

I glanced up to find Dylan watching me with a little frown.

"Will camp be canceled?" a tiny girl from Helium asked.

Goosebumps popped up on my arms. It never occurred to me that camp might be canceled permanently over the explosion.

Luis smiled. "Naw, don't worry. Maybe you will get to go home early today, but tomorrow, we will be back in action."

I hoped he was right. The last thing I wanted was camp to end before I figured out what was going on in the science building. All the incidents in Colburn must be related. They had to be.

Dylan clapped his hands and looked more like his old self. "All right, so you guys hang here for a second while we call your parents."

The four counselors moved to the second oak tree,

pulled their binders from their backpacks, and started making calls.

"Can I have the casebook?" Colin whispered. "I might as well update it while we wait."

I dug into my backpack for the casebook. I covered it with my hands as quickly as possible, glancing around at the other kids in the group to make sure no one had seen it before passing it to Colin.

Polk and Curie appeared around the side of the library. The janitor pushed a rolling cart of cleaning supplies.

Colin's glasses sat crookedly on his nose, and the tip of his tongue stuck out of his mouth while he recorded the day's events.

"Colin," I hissed.

"Hmmm?" He didn't look up from his notebook.

"Colin."

He blinked at me from behind his glasses.

"Two o'clock."

Colin found the position two o'clock from where we sat like I knew that he would. His eyes went wide and his mouth made an "o" shape.

"We have to tell him to stay away from Colburn," I breathed.

Colin gave me a slight nod.

I felt eyes on us and found Ava watching us with narrowed eyes. Luckily, just then Polk and Curie disappeared back behind the library.

"What are you two whispering about?" Ava wanted to know.

"None of your business," I snapped.

"Then, I will make it my business," she said.

I took that as a threat.

CASE FILE NO. 13

Dylan held his cell phone away from his ear as a woman on the other end shouted at him. He took a deep breath. "Yes, yes, I understand your concern, Mrs. Harper, but I can assure you that the students weren't anywhere close to the fire." He paused. "Yes, you are welcome to come and pick up Brady now if you would like." He sighed. "Okay, we will see you in a few minutes then." He hit the "end" button on his cell phone, then smoothed the crinkled piece of paper on the grass. I saw my name on the paper with Amelie's name and cell phone number. Colin's was there too with Bergita's, and so were the names and parents of the rest of those in our group. I glanced over to Madison. Her list was in a highlighted and tabbed binder.

"What is it, Andi?" Dylan asked.

I held my aunt's library books in my arms. "Would it be all right if I went to the library for a minute? I promised my aunt I would return these books for her. Since we aren't doing anything—"

His cell phone rang, and he groaned when he saw the number. "Mrs. Harper," he muttered. "Fine, fine, go return the books, but don't waste your time over there. Come straight back."

"No problem." I smiled.

He eyed me. "If you're gone more than ten minutes, you're in a heap of trouble. Why don't you take Colin with you? He can be your timekeeper."

"Okay!" I said and ran back to Colin before the counselor changed his mind. I pulled my friend to his feet.

He stumbled forward. "Where are we going?"

"To return Amelie's library books."

"I'm starting to think that is some kind of code. Every time you say 'return Amelie's library books' we go after Polk."

"Shhh! Dylan said we only have ten minutes to run to the *library*. Let's go."

He followed me across the green.

Thankfully, the main door to the library was on the opposite side of the building, so Dylan wouldn't see when we didn't go inside. I dropped Amelie's books into the book drop, and they fell into the metal container with a thunk.

"Now that you returned the books, what will you use as your Polk-spying excuse?" Colin asked.

I smiled. "I'll think of something."

As we walked back the opposite direction around

the library, we saw Polk sitting near the library's emergency exit, taking a break. Curie was at his feet.

"Polk!" Colin yelled.

Polk struggled to his feet, clutching his chest.

"Colin, you almost gave him a heart attack," I said.

"I'm sorry." Colin ran over to the older man. His backpack bounced on his back while he went. "Are you all right?"

Polk scratched his chin. "Not to worry, young man. Yes, you did startle me, but I have a strong ticker." He tiptoed down the steps to his cleaning cart and gripped the handle.

I couldn't help but wonder what was inside the cart, other than mops and cleaning supplies. Could the platinum be there? I hated to think Polk was responsible for the robbery, but I had to admit there weren't many other suspects on the list.

"Polk, we have something to tell you, but we don't have much time," I said.

"Why? What's wrong?" he asked alarmed.

Colin described the accident in the chemistry lab.

Polk reached out to Curie. "Will Meg be all right?"

The little beagle whimpered.

I awkwardly patted the older man's arm. "She's okay, Polk. An ambulance drove her to the hospital. Hopefully, we will hear soon how bad the burns are. Dylan put the fire out really quickly."

Polk's face was drawn. "There will be an investigation. It's just like it ..." he trailed off.

Colin cocked his head. "Just like what?"

"Nothing. Nothing." He shook his head like a toddler refusing food. "Meg could not be responsible for the explosion. That is a very simple and common experiment. She could have done it in her sleep. Any chemist could have."

"How do you know?" I asked.

"I—I must have remembered it from when I was in school."

My brow wrinkled. Polk must have been out of school for sixty years, if not more. He either had the world's best memory or knew more about chemistry than he let on. Maybe his knowledge of chemistry was why Dr. Comfrey allowed him in the science building after hours.

"Andi, we need to go back. Dylan said ten minutes." Colin kept looking over his shoulder as if our counselor would come looking for us at any second.

I nodded. "Polk, can you come over to Colin's house for dinner tonight?"

Colin's mouth fell open.

The janitor blinked. "That's nice of you to ask, but I wouldn't want to impose."

Colin recovered. "Bergita would love it." He removed his phone from pocket. "I can text her right now and ask."

Polk wrapped Curie's leash around his hand. "I couldn't—"

"Yes, you can," I said. "Do you have other plans?"

Polk shook his head.

Colin's phone beeped. "She says it's okay and that we are having a cookout tonight."

Polk frowned.

"Please, Bergita is expecting you," Colin said. "If you don't come, she'll be so disappointed."

"Why do I have the feeling I'm being ambushed?" Colin and I grinned.

He nodded. "Yes, I will be there if it means that the two of you will return to camp. I don't want to be held responsible for keeping you."

"Good." I paused. "And if I were you, I'd stay away from Colburn today. There are a lot of people there, including Kip. He won't be happy to see you."

Polk's face clouded over. "He never is. He has his reasons."

I hoped Polk would tell us what those reasons were at the cookout.

Colin rattled off his address. "Bergita said you should be there at five." Colin and I ran around the side of the building and almost knocked over Ava in the process.

I pulled up short. "What are you doing here?"

She placed one hand on her hip. The other held a stack of books. "I returned some library books. Is that a crime?" Ava arched an eyebrow at me. "Were you able to return your books, Andi?"

I didn't answer.

"I'd be surprised that you had enough time to run into the library since you were so busy talking to Polk."

Colin paled. "Ava, you can't tell anyone that."

She gave him a small smile before heading up the library steps.

By the time Colin and I returned to the oak tree, we had been gone thirteen minutes. Colin timed it. Fortunately, Dylan was too preoccupied by the irate parent stabbing her fingernail into his chest to notice how long we'd been gone.

The woman folded her arms. "This campus is supposed to be safe. I send my son here to learn science, and his teacher is almost killed."

Dylan was sweating. "Mrs. Harper, Dr. Comfrey will be all right. I'm sure she'll be good as new in no time."

"One of those exploding test tubes could have hit my son. He could have been burnt," she screeched.

"The kids were well back from the ex—"

"Don't make excuses."

A few feet away, Brady squirmed and looked like he wished the earth would open and swallow him.

"Mrs. Harper." Madison stepped between the angry mother and Dylan. "You have every right to be upset, but we hope you will let Brady come back to camp tomorrow. He's a bright kid, and we would hate to lose him."

Mrs. Harper's shoulders relaxed. "Yes, Brady is exceptional. He always has extremely high test scores. He's bound for the ivy league." She sniffed. "Not a shoddy university like this."

"Mom," Brady's voice jumped an octave.

Mrs. Harper smoothed the sleeve of her blouse. "We are leaving now, but Brady will be back tomorrow. I am not going to let this mishap ruin my son's chances for a scholarship someday."

Madison smiled. "I'm glad."

"I'm glad too," Dylan said.

Mrs. Harper scowled at Dylan before wrapping her arm around her son's shoulders and leading a red-faced Brady to the parking lot.

Dylan frowned. "Why did she smile pretty at you and give me the stink eye?"

Madison chuckled. "I'm the responsible one, remember?"

It was the first time I'd heard her laugh.

Other kids' parents arrived to pick up their children. I didn't see Bergita. Since Amelie was on her way to Canton with Bethany, I expected her to tell Bergita to pick us up. Colin's cell phone rang.

"Hi, Bergita," Colin said. "No, we are both fine."

"Ask her if we can go see Mr. Finnigan before going home," I said.

"Huh?"

"Just ask," I said.

Colin repeated my question to Bergita. "We should be home by dinnertime … Yes, we will help get ready for the cookout." He hung up.

"Why do you want to go see Mr. Finnigan?"

Before I could answer, Dylan slipped his phone into the back pocket of his jeans and said, "It looks like everyone from our group is either getting picked up or is headed home. Colin and Andi, you are supposed to ride your bikes to Colin's house." He checked his crinkled list. "Well, everyone is headed home except for you, Ava. I couldn't get a hold of your mom, and the guy who answered the phone said you would have to wait here until the normal time."

Ava crossed her arms. "That's fine. I don't care." She kicked the trunk of the oak tree so jagged pieces of bark fell to the ground.

I edged away from Ava and spotted Madison speaking with a middle-aged man in a suit. While Dylan and Colin were distracted by Ava, I walked over to the man and Madison.

"Obviously, you should put someone else in charge of the department," Madison said to the man. "She's making poor decisions and putting those kids in danger."

The man pinched the bridge of his nose.

"Dean Cutter, you want someone like that making decisions about the chemistry department's budget? She's making drastic cuts. Someone else on the faculty will make better choices about the budget."

"Miss Houser, if this is about the think tank for next summer, I don't want to hear it right now. I am not going to discuss the university's budgetary policies with a student." He brushed passed her. "Now, if you will excuse me."

I jumped behind a tree as he passed.

Twenty minutes later, Colin's bike coasted up alongside mine. "Now are you going to tell me why we are going to see Mr. Finnigan?"

I squeezed my bike's brakes as the brick-faced cooling tower of the old Michael Pike bottling company came into view. The bottling company closed decades ago, and now was the home of the Killdeer Historical Society and Museum. Mr. Finnigan was the town curator.

"Because if anyone in Killdeer knows the history about the university and Polk, it would be Mr. Finnigan." I kicked out my bike stand and parked the bike on the sidewalk in front of the building's front door.

Colin and I went inside. Like always, the curator sat at the too small reception desk just inside the door with his long legs stretching out in front of the desk.

"Andi! Colin! To what do I owe this pleasure?" His brow wrinkled. "I thought you two were in Discovery Camp this week," he said, proving that Mr. Finnigan knew everything that happened in Killdeer. I hoped that he knew about Polk too.

Colin sat in one of the two armchairs across from the curator's desk. "Camp was canceled for the rest of the day. There was an explosion."

Mr. Finnigan flattened his hands on the desktop and sat up suddenly, knocking his knees on the underside of the desk in the process. "*What?*"

I stopped a pencil from rolling off of the desk. "Dr.

Comfrey was hurt. She has burns on her arm. We haven't heard how bad the burns are, but she was talking to the other professors and the camp counselors when the ambulance took her away."

Mr. Finnigan leaned across the desk. "Tell me everything."

I told the curator what happened, and Colin jumped in every now and then with more details.

"Oh my, I can't believe I am just hearing about this now. I'm glad that you kids came here to tell me. As the town curator, I should be one of the first to know when something significant like this happens in Killdeer so that I can record the facts properly."

I shifted in my seat. "There's another reason we stopped by too."

"Oh?"

"What can you tell us about Polk?" I asked.

"Polk? Polk who?"

"Polk, the janitor at the university."

"Oh, you mean James Samuel Polk, no relation to the 11th president of the United States. His mother must have been unable to resist naming him James. He's worked at Michael Pike for over forty years."

"Whoa," Colin said. "Do you know his birthday too?"

The curator ran a finger over his dark mustache. "Not off hand, but I can look it up if you need it. What's your interest in Polk?"

"The explosion isn't the only strange thing going on around campus," I said. "Things have turned up missing from the chemistry lab and Kip, the security guard—"

"Yes, I know Kip too," he gestured for me to continue.

"Kip seems to think that Polk is behind it. I wouldn't be surprised if Kip thought Polk was behind the explosion too."

"There's a simple reason for that," the curator said. "Kip, full name Kipling Bart Reynolds—"

"His middle name is Bart," Colin snorted.

Mr. Finnigan just gave him a look before continuing. "Kip hates Polk. He has a grudge against him that is decades long."

"Why's that?" I asked. "What happened?"

Mr. Finnigan leaned across the desk to us. "Polk killed Kip's father."

"What?" Colin squawked before he fell out of his chair.

Colin scrambled back into his chair, and I stared at Mr. Finnigan gap-mouthed. Finally, I regained control of my voice. "What do you mean that Polk killed Kip's father?"

Mr. Finnigan leaned back into his chair. "Polk wasn't always a janitor at Michael Pike. Back in the 1970s, he was the chemistry professor there."

So that's how Polk knew so much about chemistry.

"How did Polk go from being a professor to the janitor?" Colin asked.

"I'm getting to that," Mr. Finnigan said. "Polk was a rising star in the area of chemistry. Kip's father, Doug Reynolds, was Polk's protégé. Without permission, he ran an experiment in the chemistry lab after hours. I believe the theory was he wanted to impress Polk, so that Polk would write a recommendation letter for graduate school. He was alone, and there was an explosion, a large one, not just a Bunsen burner malfunctioning like you described, and Doug was killed. He died from chemical burns."

I shivered.

"When was this?" Colin asked.

"April 1974." Mr. Finnigan pushed back from the desk. "Hang tight. I have a file on this back in the archives. It will have all the details that we need." Mr. Finnigan was back within minutes. He must have known exactly where the file was.

He fell back into his seat and put the archival folder in the middle of the desk. A newspaper article slipped out of it. "Here's an article about it from the *Cleveland Plain Dealer.* A big story like this was covered even in the big cities." He slid the clipping across the desk to Colin and me. We leaned forward to read it.

Colin ran his finger along the print. "It says that Doug was doing something with thionyl chloride. What's that?"

Mr. Finnigan shrugged. "That's a question for a chemist. Whatever it is, they think it came in contact with another chemical Doug used, which caused the explosion. Chances are if he hadn't been in the lab alone, he would have had burns but may have survived. I believe Polk found him and tried to pull him from the room, but it was too late. It is a waste. It sounds like he would have been a great scientist."

I slid the article back to Mr. Finnigan. "Did Polk go to jail?"

The curator shook his head. "No. Today, he probably would have. I'm guessing both Polk and the university would have been charged with neglect since Doug had access to the lab and conducted the experiment alone. Back in the '70s, I think the Pike family may have paid off some people to make the problem go away. They were still very much in control of the university and town then."

"Because of something that happened so long ago and something that was an accident, Kip automatically assumes that Polk is behind it?" Colin said.

"Kip and the entire Reynolds family always held Polk responsible for the tragedy even though the rumor was they took money from the Pikes too. Polk didn't cause the accident, but the college fired him from being a professor there. The Reynolds did everything in their power to make sure he didn't find another teaching job. The college felt sorry for Polk—he had been one of their star faculty members before—and offered him the janitorial job. I think everyone was surprised when he took it, and even more surprised that he has kept it so long and not found something else or moved away from Killdeer."

"Why didn't he move away?" Colin asked. "I would want to get as far away from this place as I could."

"That I don't know. You will have to ask him." The curator leaned back in his chair, and it squeaked.

We were all silent in thought. I didn't know about Colin and Mr. Finnigan, but my mind was reeling from this information. Maybe Kip took the security job at Michael Pike University because Polk was still working there. Maybe he was working there to torment Polk as some kind of forty-year-old payback, or even maybe Kip framed Polk as the ultimate payback for his father's death.

Colin stood. "Andi, we'd better go. I promised Bergita we wouldn't be long."

I raised my eyebrows at Colin. He'd told Bergita we'd be home by dinnertime. It wasn't even noon yet. I stood up too, and we thanked Mr. Finnigan and headed out to our bikes.

When we got outside, I asked, "What's the rush? Bergita doesn't expect us home for a few more hours."

"I know that, but now that we know the history between Polk and Kip, I want to get back to campus. It's the best place to learn anything about Kip. I think he has more to do with these incidents than we ever thought before. Are you in?"

Of course I was in.

Colin and I had left campus less than two hours before, but what a difference that time had made. As we cruised by the science building, I noted that the small parking lot beside Colburn was crowded with cop cars, a crime scene van, and another van that said "chemical containment" on the side of it.

"Whoa," Colin said.

My thoughts exactly.

Kip was in the middle of the parking lot talking to a cop and a guy in a hazmat suit. Dr. Comfrey with her arm in a blue sling was there, as well as Dr. Ruggles. I was so relieved to see that the chemistry professor was all right, although surprised she had returned from the hospital so quickly. They must have wanted to ask her questions. She wore a short-sleeved shirt, and a white bandage wrapped from the palm of her hand all the way to her bicep.

I worried my lip. "Do you think camp will be canceled for good?"

"I hope not. At least Dr. Comfrey looks okay."

I put my feet back up on the pedals. "We had better get out of sight. The science teachers and counselors thought we went home. I don't think they would like it if they caught us here."

Colin followed me on his bike over to the dining hall. I thought it was the best place to go. We could hide behind the building to keep out of sight from the officials swarming Colburn but still have a great vantage point to see most of the action.

Colin and I parked our bikes beside the blue dumpster that I had hid behind that morning and then returned to the corner of the building.

Suddenly, Colin pulled me backwards by my T-shirt.

I yanked my shirt away and hissed, "What?"

He didn't say a word, just pointed. The camp counselors and Ava stepped out of the cafeteria's side door. Colin and I ducked behind the dumpster.

Madison folded her arms and unknowingly turned her back to Colin and me. "I don't know why they won't let me over to help the crime scene guys. I know as much chemistry as anyone else, even those wannabe biohazard officers."

"Someone has to stay with Ava." Susan snapped her gum.

"We don't all have to be with her. Kip used that as an excuse to get rid of us."

Ava folded her arms. "I don't need to be babysat. I'd be fine by myself in the library until my brother gets here."

"See," Madison said. "And I shouldn't have to spend

my summer babysitting any of these kids," Madison snapped. "I should be in DC."

"Ugh," Susan said. "Madison, you hold a grudge, girl. If I hear one more word about your 'woe is me' story and how you were forced to work at this camp, I'm going to hurl."

"Me too," Luis agreed.

"You two are just jealous because you never even had a shot."

Colin and I shared a look.

"Wrong. Some of us are working at camp because we actually like kids," Luis said. "Dr. Comfrey should have never put you in charge."

"Who was she going to put in charge then? One of you? If you like kids so much then go be a kindergarten teacher."

Ava scowled and sat on a step. She removed one of her lab notebooks from her bag and started writing.

"Dylan, don't you think I deserve more than this?" Madison asked.

Dylan glanced up from his smart phone. "You know I do, Madison." He frowned and dropped his gaze.

"You guys can stay here with Ava. I have work to do." Madison walked away, clutching her clipboard to her chest.

Susan snorted. "Like we are going to take Dylan's word for it. Madison could tell him the moon was made of popcorn, and he'd believe it."

"No, I wouldn't." Dylan half-grinned. "It's made of cheese, right?" He ran after Madison.

Susan groaned. "Oh, hey, Ava, tell your mom I said

thanks. She did a great job getting that tar stain out of my favorite pair of jeans."

Ava's jaw twitched.

Luis held up two fingers. "Two questions. One, how did you get tar on your jeans, and two, what does Ava's mom have to do with it?"

"The first one is a long story, but Ava's mom is my family's maid." She smiled brightly at Ava. "She must be so proud of you for making it into Discovery Camp. What an achievement!"

Ava looked up from her notebook. "Does it surprise you that I'm smart when my mother's a maid?"

Susan turned bright red. "No, of course not. I didn't mean it like that."

Ava slammed her notebook. "Then how did you mean it?"

Susan didn't answer.

Ava stood. "Not all of us have rich parents. The only chance I will have to go to a college like this one is with a scholarship. Don't rub it in my face."

Susan's mouth fell open. "Ava—"

"I'm going to the library. Don't come with me." She stomped away.

"Nice work, Susan," Luis said.

"I was trying to be nice. I thought she would like to hear something nice about her mom. Ava's not the easiest to talk to." She folded her arms. "She reminds me of Madison."

Luis shook his head. "Let's go. We can hang out by Colburn, and maybe find out if there will be camp tomorrow."

The two college students walked away from the library.

"What are you two staring at?" a voice asked behind Colin and me.

We both jumped.

Polk stood a few feet behind us. Curie sat at his feet. Her leash lay on the ground. The beagle waddled in the direction of the dumpster.

I swallowed, looking at Polk differently now that I knew about the previous campus explosion.

"Hi, Polk," Colin squeaked.

He smiled. "You were listening to those kids, weren't you?" His shoulder sagged. "They must think I caused the accident this morning. Everyone else on campus does."

"They didn't say anything about you," Colin said. "They were complaining that they still have to work today when most of the kids went home."

Polk snorted. "I'm used to kids like Madison. Entitled."

Behind Polk, I just saw the hint of black and white fur around the corner. This was bad.

I cleared my throat. "Umm, Polk, you'd better get Curie. I saw a baby skunk over here this morning. She might get in trouble."

All three of us headed to Curie to pull the dog away from the baby skunk's hiding place. Curie happily snuffled the ground. We were within three feet of Curie when the skunk came around the corner, but it wasn't the little baby skunk that I had seen before. It was the big mama, and she wasn't happy. She turned tail and hit us with both barrels. I covered my face in the nick of time. From his screams, Colin wasn't so lucky.

Curie began to howl. I lowered my hands. The smell was overwhelming. The beagle had taken the brunt of the skunk's spray, but the rest of us hadn't been spared. I gagged. "What do we do now?"

"Let's go to my house," Colin said with his hand over his nose and mouth. "Polk, you should come too."

The older man looked down at his dog. "Poor Curie. I get off work at three. I don't think the boss will care if I take off a little bit early under the circumstances. It's not like I can clean any of the buildings in this condition."

"How are we going to leave campus without walking by the science building?" I asked. Colburn was the closest building to the main entrance. "There are police and campus officials there. They are sure to see us, and if they can't see us, they are sure to smell us."

"There is a service exit we can use. It's closed to students, and the university uses it for deliveries," Polk said. "Get your bikes and follow me."

The walk to the Carters' house was terrible. We smelled awful, and we knew it, and we were constantly reminded of it as drivers rolled up their car windows to block the smell.

"This is a new low," Colin said as we stumbled up his driveway.

Bergita threw open the front door. "You're ho— Yack! What a stink!"

I hung my head. "Skunk."

"I can smell it," she said in a muffled voice because she covered most of her mouth. "To the backyard with the four of you. Don't even set foot on this porch."

We stumbled down the driveway to the backyard. I unlatched the fence.

Jackson and Bergita appeared at the house's back door. Jackson took two steps into the backyard, lifted his nose, and bolted between Bergita's legs back into the house. Bergita started giving orders. "Colin, grab the kiddie pool we use for Jackson's baths. It's leaning against the back of the garage."

"What's the kiddie pool for?" Polk asked.

"You," Bergita said.

Colin rolled the blue plastic wading pool into the middle of the yard and dropped it.

"Get in, all of you. I'll be right back." Bergita disappeared into the house. Seconds later, she returned with a manual can opener in one hand and three extra-large cans of V8 and one can of stewed tomatoes in the other. A wooden clothespin pinched her nose closed.

"This was all I had, but it will get you started." She pulled up short. "Why aren't you in the pool?" Her voice sounded stuffy because of the clothespin.

Colin and I hopped into the pool. Polk, holding Curie, lowered himself in. We settled into our spots. It was a tight fit, but we made it work.

Bergita started opening the cans of V8. "You might want to take your phones out of your pockets."

We all emptied our pockets, and Bergita poured V8 on our heads.

"Yow!" Colin shivered. "That's cold!"

Polk wiped V8 from his deep-set eyes. "This is not the way to deal with a skunking. What you need is hydrogen peroxide, baking soda, and liquid soap. Tomato juice will only cover the smell."

Bergita poured an entire can on Curie. The beagle howled. Polk had to keep a firm grip on her.

Bergita shook the last drop from the can of stewed tomatoes. "How do you know?" Bergita asked.

Polk swallowed. "I—I saw it on television."

Bergita cocked her head. "I'm willing to give it a try if it will work. But I don't have enough hydrogen peroxide in the house for this job. You all sit there and marinate for a while. I'm going to have to run to the market. I'll pick up some tomato juice too just to be safe." She eyed us. "When I get back, you are going to tell me how you got into this predicament."

After Bergita left, I turned to Polk. V8 dripped from my nose. "How do you know about the hydrogen peroxide, Polk? I don't believe it's from television."

The older man shifted uncomfortably.

Curie shook her head and tomato juice flew into the

air. *Curie*. I had never thought about her name before. "You named your dog after Marie Curie, the scientist."

Polk wiped V8 from the wrinkles on his cheek. He still had a firm grip on Curie with his other hand. "Why, yes, I did."

"Because you used to be a chemist," I said. "You were the chemistry professor at the university a long time ago."

Polk frowned. "How do you know that?"

"We asked a friend," Colin said.

Curie wiggled in her master's lap and pulled Polk's glove from his wrist in the process. I got just a glimpse of a scar on the back of his hand. "It's okay, girl. This will take the smell away."

I swallowed. "Is that scar from the explosion in the chemistry lab when you were a professor there, and a student died?"

"Who told you that?" He yanked up his glove and tightened his grip on Curie.

She whimpered.

He relaxed. "I'm sorry, old girl."

"Mr. Finnigan at the historical society told us." Colin shook tomato juice from his glasses. I bet he wished he had thought to take them off before Bergita started pouring the V8.

Polk nodded. "Yes, Patrick would know. He knows everything about everyone in the town."

"So it's true?" Colin said.

"I won't deny it. That event made me the person I am today." His voice dropped. "For good or ill."

"The student who died was Kip's father."

He nodded. "I see you've done your homework. Kip

never liked me because of his father's death. Now, he believes he has the ammunition to get rid of me for good. Before you ask, I had nothing to do with the accident in Meg's lab. I wouldn't do anything that might put Meg in jeopardy like that. She is a talented chemist and has a bright future. I don't want hers to be stolen like mine was."

"Is she a relative of yours?" Colin asked.

The older man shook his head. "No. But she is kind, and when she learned about what had happened to me she opened the lab to me. She said I could visit as much as I liked. I appreciated that. For so long, I was told to stay away from the chemistry lab. To be welcomed back was a nice change. Of course, I had been in the lab many times in the intervening years as part of my job, but to be welcomed back not as the *help* but as a colleague, as someone to be consulted with over lesson plans and lab experiments—it was wonderful. I felt like my old self again, something I had lost all those years ago when a mistake destroyed my life." He sighed. "And I know I am not the one who suffered the greatest loss. Doug, the student who died, and his young wife and baby son, Kip did. He was a bright student, and I mourned his loss too."

As Polk spoke, his grasp on Curie must have loosened because before we knew it, the dog wiggled out of his grasp and dashed for the gate Bergita had left open in her haste to buy more tomato juice. As Curie ran, stewed tomatoes and droplets of V8 juice trailed behind her. She disappeared through the gate.

Polk, Colin, and I scrambled to our feet, but the tomato-slick kiddie pool was too slippery, and we landed in a heap. Finally, I was able to roll out of the pool onto the grass and landed on my back like a turtle. My shoelace caught on the lip of the pool. It took me precious seconds to unravel it.

Polk didn't wait and hurried through the gate by the time I made it to my feet.

"Are you okay?" Colin asked.

"I'm fine. Go find Polk and Curie." I quickly tied my shoes, which wasn't that easy with laces coated in tomato.

Colin shot through the gate.

By the time I got out on the driveway, Polk, Colin, and Curie were gone, but it wasn't hard to see which way they went. I just had to follow the tomato paw prints. They led me to the end of the street and a house on the corner. Polk watched the house anxiously.

I caught my breath as I stared at the house. "What's going on?"

"Curie is under the porch, and Colin went under there after him."

"Have the owners come out?"

He shook his head and a stewed tomato went flying into the grass. "Colin knocked on the door to see if they were home, but no one answered."

I dug my fingernails into my palms. Colin should have waited for me and let me crawl under the porch.

There was bound to be all sorts of things he was allergic to under there. I didn't want him to have an asthma attack. I peeked under the house. "Colin?"

"I'm okay," he wheezed. "I have Curie. We're coming out."

The white of his tomato-streaked sneakers caught the light as he wiggled backwards toward the opening. His feet and legs appeared. He was about halfway out when I saw Curie's muddy head. Someone was going to need a bath. That was for sure.

"Hold on," I said. "Wait right there for a second." I ran back to Polk and grabbed Curie's leash from him. I clicked it on her collar and pulled her out the rest of the way. "I got her. Come on out."

Colin wriggled backwards and rolled onto his back. His hair was plastered to his head. Mud and tomato juice covered his arms and legs. I could barely see the camp logo on his T-shirt.

I started to giggle. "You look like you mud wrestled a tomato."

Colin picked a stewed tomato out of his hair. "The tomato won."

Polk knelt beside Curie. He gave the dog a bear hug. "Shhh, shhh, you are okay, girl. You're just fine."

The dog gave him a big sloppy kiss up one side of Polk's face and down the other, and the former chemist laughed. It was a deep belly laugh, and it hit me like a slap. It sounded so much like my father's laugh, I staggered backward.

"Are you okay, Andi?" Colin's face was streaked with tomato and mud. I couldn't have looked much better.

I shook thoughts of my parents away. "I'm okay."

Colin brushed his bangs off of his dirty glasses and blinked at me from behind the dirty lenses. "Are you sure?"

"Why wouldn't I be?" I asked a little too quickly.

Colin frowned. "Bergita's not going to be happy."

Polk stood and placed a hand on his back. "Maybe I should leave. I don't want to cause trouble for you with your grandmother."

"You have to come back," Colin wheezed. "She will want to make sure Curie is okay for herself, and what about all the tomato juice and hydrogen peroxide she is buying?" He wheezed again. This wasn't good.

I scrunched up my face and studied Colin. "You feel okay? Maybe you should take some puffs of your inhaler."

He tapped his shorts pocket and his shoulders drooped. "It's back in the yard. I took it out of my pocket to save it from the tomato juice."

"We'd better head back then," I said.

"All right, we will come." Polk petted Curie's head. "I hope your grandmother is back with the ingredients we need."

The dog was covered in mud and tomato. A bath was in order for all of us. At least it was a hot summer day, and I wouldn't mind getting soaked again.

We headed back to the house. Bergita stood in the middle of the driveway with hands on her hips. Two crates of tomato juice and the largest bottle of hydrogen peroxide I'd ever seen sat on the driveway beside her. "What on earth is going on?"

"My apologies, Bergita. It is my fault. I let Curie

loose, and she ran to a neighbor's house. She crawled underneath their porch. Colin got her out for me."

Bergita's typical sunny expression clouded over. "Colin did what? Who knows how many allergens could be lurking under a house—mold, dust, just to name a few. Not to mention, the heat can set off an asthma attack." She held up his inhaler, "You are running around and I find *this* in the backyard."

Colin coughed and took the inhaler from his grandmother. He took two quick puffs. Seconds later his shoulders relaxed.

"What do you have to say for yourself?"

"I'm sorry," Colin winced. "Andi reminded me to take it."

"Good. I'm glad one of you has some sense. I don't mind the skunk attack, but asthma attacks are a whole different story. I won't tolerate one of those, young man, especially when they can be avoided with a bit of common sense."

"I'm sorry," Colin muttered.

Bergita gave a curt nod. "Apology accepted, but I don't want to hear about you doing something like that again. Understand me?"

"Yes," Colin squeaked.

"Good. Now, take this tomato juice and hydrogen peroxide to the backyard and get into the pool. I will grab some baking soda, soap, and towels from inside the house. Then I will start up the grill for our cookout. I want everything to be relatively normal by the time your aunt gets home, Andi." She paused. "And you still don't smell so good."

An hour later, I sat on Bergita's back porch, toweling

my hair dry. After the tomato juice and hydrogen peroxide mixture soaking, Bergita thought I smelled okay enough to run over to my house and shower. I lathered up with half a bottle of my sister's favorite Bath and Body Works body wash. She would be mad, but I would buy her another bottle. The regular soap I typically used wasn't going to cut it. At the moment I smelled like Japanese Cherry Blossom with just a hint of skunk. Polk had been right. The hydrogen peroxide mixture worked much better than the tomato juice. I hoped the smell would all wear off in time for camp tomorrow—*if* there was camp tomorrow.

Colin was inside his house cleaning up, and Polk sat on another patio chair wearing a borrowed T-shirt and sweatpants from Colin's dad's closet. Despite the heat and the fact that they were soaking, Polk wore his leather gloves.

Curie, who suffered the direct hit, still smelled a little funky, but we silently agreed to ignore it. She lay in the now empty kiddie pool.

Colin came through the back door. His hair, which was usually in his face, was damp and slicked back.

Bergita piled hamburgers from the grill onto a plate. "Everyone go ahead and dig in. Bethany called while you were all cleaning up to tell us not to wait and eat. She and Amelie were going to grab something at the mall."

That was probably for the best.

I poured glasses of lemonade. "It's not just Bethany. They went there to pick up Bethany's best friend from back home, Kaylee."

"That's even better." Bergita nodded. "I know

Bethany misses her old life. It will be good for her to see her friend."

"It was Amelie's idea."

Bergita smiled. "She's coming into her own with this parenting thing. It took some time, but she's finally getting the hang of it."

I wanted to ask Bergita what she meant by that, but before I could say anything, she clapped her hands. "Let's eat before the burgers get cold."

Colin and Polk loaded their burgers with every condiment from Bergita's kitchen. Barbeque sauce, mayo, relish, ketchup, mustard, and who knew what else. As I just added mustard and a pickle to my burger, I decided that it must be a guy thing, no matter what the age of the guy was. Not that I knew how old Polk was, but he had to be at least as old as Bergita, and Colin told me once she was seventy-six. After telling me, he swore me to secrecy because Bergita wouldn't like it. She tells everyone that she is fifty-nine.

Polk arranged potato salad, carrots, and fruit on his plate. He lifted his fork to his mouth.

"Let's say grace before we start eating," Bergita said. She said a short blessing, and then poured herself a glass of iced tea. "Tell me about the skunk from the beginning."

Colin was in the middle of telling his grandmother about the day's adventure when my aunt's voice rang over the fence. "Hello, hello. We're home!"

Amelie unlatched the gate and came through. I expected to see my sister and Kaylee with her, but they weren't there.

Amelie smiled. "Bethany took Kaylee in the house

to show her around and to compare their shopping finds." She blew out a breath. "Whew, those girls can shop. We must have gone into every teen store in the mall. My feet are killing me. I think some relaxing yoga is in order to restore my balance." She pulled up short. "Oh, you have company."

"Good evening, Amelie," Polk said.

"Amelie, have you met Polk before?" I asked.

"Of course. It's nice to see you off campus, Polk. Andi mentioned that she met you during camp." She sat on an empty chair on the deck and kicked off her Birkenstocks. "So how was camp today? And why are the three of you," she paused, "and Curie wet? And what's that smell?"

"Camp went okay until the explosion," Colin said.

Amelie bolted straight up in her chair. "What? What explosion?"

I propped my face in my hands. "You might want to sit back to hear this."

After a couple of minutes of explaining what happened, we were finally able to calm Amelie down.

"That's it. I'm buying a car charger for my cell phone," Amelie said. "Halfway to Canton, I realized the battery was dead, but I thought we would be okay since Bethany had her phone. I bet when I plug in mine, I will find a message from the camp about this. Some guardian I turned out to be." She dropped her head in her hands.

Bergita clicked her tongue. "Don't beat yourself up. Part of learning to parent is making mistakes. Lots of them. If I had thought that Colin and Andi were in any danger, I would have run over to campus and fetched them."

The cell phone in Bergita's shorts pocket rang. She

fished it out. "Hello?" She nodded even though the person on the other end couldn't see her. "That's good to hear. Yes, definitely, they will both be there tomorrow."

I sat up straight.

Bergita snapped her phone closed. "Good news. Camp is back on for tomorrow."

Amelie frowned. "I don't know that I want Andi going back after that explosion."

"Bah." Bergita waved away her concern. "The kids will be fine. Besides, the kid I spoke to said that the chemistry lab would be closed for the next couple of days. Andi and Colin won't even be allowed to go in that room."

My aunt picked at her thumbnail. "If you think it's safe enough for Colin, then I guess Andi can go too. Not that I won't worry."

"Worry is part of the job of child rearing."

Amelie stood up from her lawn chair. "Thanks, Bergita. It's been a long day, and I'm pooped. Andi, you ready to go home?"

I hesitated. I didn't want to leave if there was a chance that Colin and I could learn more from Polk.

Polk struggled to his feet. "Curie and I should head home as well." He nodded to Bergita. "Thank you for a lovely dinner." He turned to Colin and me. "And thanks to the two of you for giving Curie a bath." He smiled. "Twice."

"Where do you live?" Colin blurted out.

I was relieved that he asked the question because I was about to ask it myself.

"I have a little house not far from campus."

Bergita stood. "Let me grab my car keys, and I will give you a lift there."

He shook his head. "Thank you for the offer, but I would rather walk. Walking is what keeps these old bones moving." He eyed Curie. "And I don't want Curie to stink up your car. It might be a few days before she smells normal again."

After Polk shuffled down the driveway, Amelie headed home too. She turned when I didn't follow. "Andi, let's go so you can say hello to Kaylee."

"Be there in a minute," I called from the Carters' driveway.

Colin held Jackson, who had decided to join us when the burgers were on the grill. The squat pug was a heavy load, but Colin didn't seem to mind. "I think we got some good information out of Polk tonight."

I tucked a frizzy lock of hair behind my ear. "But there's something about this older explosion Polk isn't telling us, and it might lead to some answers about the one that happened today. We need to talk to Dr. Comfrey."

He nodded. "And Kip too."

"Good idea," I said.

Bergita whistled from the front door. "Colin Carter, say good night. You will see Andi tomorrow."

Colin waved and ran into his house with Jackson bouncing on his hip.

As soon as I stepped into the house, I heard giggling. It took me a second to realize that it was my sister laughing. I hadn't heard my sister genuinely laugh since we moved to Killdeer, maybe even since our parents died. I smiled at the sound. Amelie was right; having Kaylee visit had been a great idea.

Footsteps pounded down the stairs, and Bethany and Kaylee skidded to a stop at the first floor.

"Hi, Andi," Kaylee said, smiling brightly. Her face fell. "What happened to you?"

"Did you roll in a mud puddle or something?" Bethany asked.

I touched the top of my head. I thought I had washed all the mud out of my hair.

Kaylee grinned and showed off her perfectly straight and white teeth—her father was a dentist. "I guess you've really gone country, Andi." Her friendly smile took the bite out of her words.

Bethany giggled.

"I gave a friend's dog a bath. It was messy work," I said. There was no point mentioning the skunk. Bethany would freak out at the skunk.

"I guess," Kaylee said as she tugged on her sleek black ponytail. What I wouldn't give for Kaylee's hair, which was board straight, a gift from her Vietnamese father. When Kaylee wakes up, her ebony locks are perfect. Kaylee had spent enough sleepovers at our house over the years that I knew it for a fact.

Bethany flopped on the couch. "You got dirty from giving Jackson a bath? He's only a pug, not a Great Dane."

"It wasn't Jackson." I dropped my camp backpack by the front door. "It's a beagle named Curie. He belongs to Polk, this old guy that hangs out around the university."

Bethany just shook her head as if she didn't understand me at all. Kaylee fell onto the couch next to my sister. "Who's Jackson then?"

"He's our next-door neighbor's dog," Bethany

answered. "He belongs to Colin. He's the boy that Andi likes, the one I told you about."

I folded my arms. "Colin is my *friend*."

Bethany grinned, and she and Kaylee shared a smirk. My happiness over my sister's laughter vanished.

Amelie entered the living room and rolled out her yoga mat in the middle of the floor. "Girls, maybe you should start taking yoga to settle your chi."

Bethany wrinkled her nose. "No thanks." She stood up and grabbed Kaylee by the hand. "Let's go up to my room and try on our new outfits."

Kaylee popped off of the couch, and the pair ran upstairs. Mr. Rochester raced up the stairs after them. I thought it was the mention of the new clothes that got the orange tabby moving. There was nothing Mr. Rochester like more than to take a nap in a basket of clean laundry.

Amelie, who sat on her knees on the yoga mat, frowned as she watched them go up the stairs.

"What's wrong, Amelie?" I asked.

She put her feet out in front of her and reached for her toes.

I thought she wasn't going to answer me, but Amelie surprised me. "I have never seen your sister so happy, genuinely happy." She nibbled on her bottom lip. "Maybe I'm doing the wrong thing by making her live here. Maybe I should let her live with the Cragmeyers."

I chewed on the inside of my lip. Amelie couldn't be serious. Bethany and I fought, but she couldn't leave me here alone. She was all I had left from my mom and dad.

Amelie sighed and bent at the waist staring at her

knees. It was like living with a human pretzel. "Were Colin's parents home for any part of the cookout?"

I fell onto the spot of the couch Kaylee had left, shaking my head. "Nope."

"I guess that's for the best. They wouldn't be thrilled with Polk being there or the tomato bath, but poor Colin, I feel for the kid."

"I know what it's like," I muttered.

Amelie spun around to face me. "What do you mean?"

"It's nothing."

She cocked her head. "It didn't sound like nothing."

I pulled at a loose thread on one of the throw pillows. If I tugged too hard the entire seam would come undone. "It's just I know what it's like, both Bethany and I do. Mom and Dad weren't home a lot. They had really important jobs."

"They did," she agreed.

Before I could stop myself, I said, "And they loved their jobs more than Bethany and me."

Tears gathered in the corners of my aunt's eyes. "Is that what you think?"

"No … Maybe."

She pulled her knees up to her chest. "Do you know what your father talked about when we spoke?"

I shook my head, refusing to look at her. More of the pillow's thread came loose.

"You and Bethany. I don't think he said one word about his research or his plants since Bethany and you were born. All he talked about was you girls, and how proud he and your mom were of you. He talked about your science projects and Bethany's paintings." She laughed. "He spoke about your schoolwork so much I felt like I was doing it with you. He *never* talked about his job."

I dropped the thread. "Is that true?"

She nodded. "Yes. Your mom and dad loved you and Bethany so much. I know that they were busy, but you and Bethany were most important to them." She searched my face. "Do you believe me?"

I nodded. If I said anything, I would start crying. I didn't want to do that. I wouldn't be able to stop.

"Good, and since we are sharing fears, I'll tell you one of my own. Knowing how much your parents loved you definitely puts the pressure on me. I don't want to screw you girls up." Her voice dropped to just above a whisper.

"You're doing all right," I managed to say.

She laughed. "Thanks for the vote of confidence, and I hope you're right. When it comes to Bethany, I'm not sure." She turned ninety degrees and stretched her legs out in front of herself again on the yoga mat. "I shouldn't make such a big decision where Bethany is concerned when I'm tired. I will have to think about this and do what I think is best for your sister and for our family." She met my eyes, still not knowing how much the idea of Bethany leaving terrified me. "Don't tell your sister that I said this. I don't want to get her hopes up."

I swallowed. "I won't tell her," I said, deciding not to say anything about my worries about Bethany leaving. Sharing one big fear about my family was enough for that night.

I yawned while Colin and I chained our bikes to the bike rack outside of Colburn the next morning.

"That's the fifth time you've yawned since we left home. Why are you so tired?"

I yawned again. "Bethany and Kaylee were up all night listening to music. I didn't get a wink of sleep. Amelie could sleep through a hurricane, so it didn't bother her."

He blew at his floppy brown hair. "Why didn't you tell them to be quiet?"

"I did, like four times. They thought it was funny." I yawned again. "I wonder if we will have chemistry this morning with the lab closed."

Colin shrugged.

"Hey, kids," Dylan greeted. "Glad to see you came back."

My forehead wrinkled. "Why wouldn't we come back?"

His sunny expression faded a couple of watts. "Because of what happened yesterday. Madison said some parents pulled their kids out of the camp."

"That's dumb," Colin said.

Dylan cracked a smile. "I totally agree with you."

Madison came up the walk, carrying a box of supplies. "Everyone inside," she ordered. "I don't want any mishaps today." She gave Colin and me a beady look. "And that goes for campers wandering off too. I know about your escapade yesterday."

Colin's eyes widened.

Madison could be scary when she was in teacher-mode. If anyone had the right personality to be a principal, it was Madison.

Without argument, Colin and I followed Dylan and Madison into the science building. I wondered if Dr. Comfrey would show up today.

We went into the lecture hall. All the other campers—or the ones whose parents didn't pull them out—were there. Susan and Luis were in the front of the room talking to Kip the security guard. He was a surprise to see in the lecture hall.

Madison went to the front of the room to talk to Kip. Before he could follow her, I tugged on Dylan's sleeve. "What's Kip doing here?"

The counselor cocked an eyebrow. "Should I be alarmed that you are on a first name basis with Michael Pike's head of security?"

I released his sleeve. "Nope."

Dylan went to the front of the room without answering me. Colin and I sat in the back with the rest of Hydrogen. Everyone was there except Brady. I guessed his mother pulled him out after all.

Ava stacked her notebooks, one for each lab, in front of her. I couldn't forget the conversation I overheard between her and Susan yesterday, and I wondered when her brother finally came to take her home. She caught me looking and glared.

In the front of the room, Madison gripped her clipboard so hard that her knuckles turned white. "Welcome back, campers. I know yesterday didn't go exactly as planned, but I promise you, today will be a great day with no mishaps." She glanced at Kip, who stood next to her. His hands were folded across his chest. "Some of you may know Kip Reynolds. He is the head of security on campus and asked to say a few words to you before we get started." Madison stepped to the side.

"Thank you, Madison. And I would thank you kids if you could give me your full attention for the next couple of minutes."

The class leaned forward.

"As you know we had an incident yesterday in the chemistry lab. Thankfully, no one was severely hurt. Dr. Comfrey suffered second degree burns on her left hand and arm, but it could have been much worse. The university is taking a close look at this situation." Kip hiked up his pants. "If any of you know anything about how this may have happened, I am asking you to come forward."

Spenser raised his hand. "You think the fire wasn't an accident?"

"I am not at liberty to say, but we are investigating all possibilities," Kip said.

"Is there a reward or something?" Chase asked.

Kip scowled. "Doing the right thing is its own reward."

Chase wrinkled his nose.

"We've received some excellent tips from some of your classmates, which have been helpful. It also makes me believe that the rest of you might know something about the incident as well."

I sat very still because I suspected any squirming would attract Kip's attention, and that's the last thing I wanted. Colin cast his eyes down on his desk. Ahh, the old don't-make-eye contact-to-avoid-being-called-on trick. It was a classic.

"Also, we are looking for Polk. He wandered off yesterday afternoon before the end of his shift and has not returned. Both campus security and the Killdeer police find this behavior highly suspicious."

Polk didn't show up for work? What happened when he left Colin's house last night?

Kip widened his stance and placed his hands behind his back, soldier-style. "I'm sure you are all familiar with him as he has been a fixture around Colburn all week." His eyes scanned the room. "Some of you are more familiar with him than others, I understand."

Uh-oh. I had a sinking feeling in the pit of my stomach.

Dylan stood behind the guard. His eyes were

downcast on the floor. He didn't mimic Kip or even make a funny face. He just stared at the floor.

"Taking into account Polk's recent behavior and his history," — Kip said "history" as if he were saying a dirty word — "we want you to keep an eye out for him."

The sinking feeling in my stomach formed into a knot. Beside me, Colin gasped.

Kip let his eyes travel across the room of campers. "If *any* of you, any of you at all, have any information about Polk and where he might be, you must bring it forward. Does anyone have anything to share?"

No one moved for fear of being caught in Kip's laser beam stare. No one said a word.

Kip grunted. "This is what I was afraid of. It would be easier if you came forward and told me what you know."

Ava raised her hand.

Madison stepped forward again. "Yes, Ava, do you know something?"

Ava sat straight in her seat. "No, but I know there are some kids in camp who spend a lot of time with Polk."

Colin shifted in his seat. I bit my lip.

"And who is that?" Kip asked.

Ava turned to glance back at me. She smiled broadly. "Maybe you should ask Andi."

In the front of the room, Dylan's head snapped up when my name was spoken.

Ava folded her hands on the tabletop like a model student. "And Colin too, since they are always together."

Colin's mouth fell open. A phrase that Bethany liked jumped into my head. "Thrown under the bus." Well, at least I knew what that felt like now.

Kip nodded. "Thank you, Ava. We realize how difficult that must have been to turn in your classmates."

Yeah, right. Really difficult.

Kip scanned the room. "Where can I find Andi and Colin?"

As if on cue, Colin and I sunk in our seats. The movement attracted Kip's attention.

"Andi, Colin, stand up," Madison said.

Colin swallowed hard like an ice cube got stuck in his throat. Slowly we both stood.

Kip frowned. "I'm going to need to talk to both of them now."

Dylan stepped forward for the first time. "Is that necessary? They are just kids. What could they know?"

"They've been seen with Polk recently. That's the only reason I need to question them."

Madison folded her arms. "Go on, you two, and talk to Kip. After you are done, Hydrogen will be meeting back here in the lecture hall for the first lab. The chem lab and the second floor are strictly off limits. Dr. Comfrey is here and she will lecture from this room. There will be no more chemical experiments during camp, although that should go without saying."

Kip walked to the door at the front of the room. "Andi, Colin, come with me."

Colin and I hesitated.

"I have no time for nonsense," Kip growled.

Behind me I heard Gavin whisper to Spenser, "Does he remind you of a bear?"

"Yeah," Spenser whispered back. "A grizzly."

Great. Colin and I were going to be questioned by a grizzly.

"I don't have all day," Kip said. "The sooner we talk, the sooner you can go back to camping or whatever it is you all are doing here."

Colin's and my chairs scraped the linoleum flooring as we pushed them under the table. I felt the eyes of the entire camp on our backs as we stumbled down the tiered classroom to the door where Kip stood. Colin went first out of the door, and just before I followed him, I glanced back up to Hydrogen. Ava gave me a broad smile and a wink. Seventh grade would be a killer.

"Let's go outside," the security guard said.

Colin and I followed him out of the building through a side door that I hadn't even known was there. I glanced at Colin and willed him not to say too much about Polk to Kip.

Kip stood under the shade of a maple tree. "Tell me what you know. How do you know Polk?"

"He's a janitor here," I said.

"You must know him better than that to have your friend share your names."

I folded my arms. "Ava is not my friend."

Kip ground his teeth. "I have no interest in your junior high drama. If she is not your friend, why would she say that?"

"To cause trouble," Colin said.

The security guard shook his head. "There's more to it than that. She saw you with Polk."

"I don't see why it is any of your business," Colin said, trying to look tough, but then his glasses slid down the bridge of his nose.

"It's my business because of the series of disturbing events that have taken place on campus the last several days, most notably the explosion in the chemistry lab. We have reason to believe that someone deliberately tampered with the Bunsen burner with the intention to hurt Dr. Comfrey and the children—meaning you—in that class. It's a serious offense. We have even more reason to believe that Polk was behind it."

"Why?" I asked. "Because of your dad?"

Kip stepped back. "Did Polk tell you about it? What is it, something that he is proud of? A tale to entertain little children? He confessed to the crime."

I let the little children comment slide. "He didn't confess to any crime," I snapped. "Polk didn't tell us. We found out on our own."

"However you know about it, that doesn't change that you need to tell me if you know where Polk is."

"We don't know." Sweat gathered on Colin's forehead. "Honest. We haven't seen him since last night."

I suppressed a groan.

Kip jumped on it. "Last night? What were you doing with him last night?"

"Ooops," Colin whispered.

"He came to a cookout at Colin's house," I said. "It wasn't a big deal."

"I'll be the judge of that, and I will call your parents. If you withhold information, you will be banned from this campus." He glared at me. "You wouldn't want to do anything that would jeopardize your aunt's position."

I glared at him. "My aunt wasn't even at the cookout. She only saw him for a few minutes at the end."

Kip sucked on his two front teeth. "Polk is a dangerous man. He has a vendetta against the university and no concern for human life."

If anyone had a grudge against Michael Pike University, it was Kip, not Polk.

"A vendetta? For being demoted to janitor?" Colin frowned. "Why would he wait forty years to get his revenge?"

"I—I don't know," Kip stuttered. His dark brows fused together and looked like a black caterpillar on his face. "I thought I was the one supposed to be asking the questions around here. Why were you two with Polk in the first place?"

"We were giving his dog a bath," I said.

Kip's mouth fell open. "What?"

Colin cleaned his glasses on the hem of his T-shirt before putting them back. "Curie had a run-in with a skunk, so we offered to give her a bath. We went to my house. You can call my grandma Bergita if you don't believe it. She was there. Actually, we gave him two baths. The dog escaped in the middle of the first one and got dirty again."

Kip's mouth hung open. "That's it? You gave his dog a bath."

"Pretty much," I said.

"Are you in the habit of giving strangers' dogs baths?"

"Polk's not a stranger," Colin said. "Bergita knows him."

Kip closed his eyes for a moment. "This is why I don't work with elementary school children."

"We are not in elementary school," I snapped.

Kip ran a hand through his hair. "During the dog bath, did Polk say anything to you about the explosion?"

I shrugged. "Just what Colin already told you about the explosion forty years ago. What's been happening lately has brought back bad memories for him."

"I would *hate* for him to have bad memories. My childhood was full of bad memories because of him, because he allowed my father in that lab alone."

I stepped back from his anger. "I know your dad—"

"You don't know any of it. I was just a baby when my father died. My mother was young and scared and married the first man she could after dad's death." He balled his hands into fists. "My stepfather was not a good man." He blinked as if pushing a memory into the back of his mind. "Excuse me if I don't feel sorry for Polk's bad memories. I have a lifetime of my own."

Colin and I didn't say a word, but I no longer saw a grumpy security guard in front of me. He was a hurt kid.

Kip pointed at us. "If I find out the two of you are withholding information, you will be sorry."

I put my hands on my hips. "I don't know much about being a university security guard, but I'm pretty sure you're not supposed to threaten students."

"You are not a university student."

"They aren't," Dylan said. "But I am."

I turned. He stood at Colburn's side door and held it open. "Give them a break, Kip. They are just a couple of twelve-year-old kids. They don't know anything about Polk or about the explosion. And they are late for their chemistry lesson."

"Fine," Kip said. "They are free to go." He pointed at his eyes with two fingers and then at Colin and me. "But I am watching you two." Kip hiked up his pants and sauntered off.

Colin and I walked to the side door.

"Are you two okay?" Dylan asked.

I nodded.

He gave a half-hearted smile. "Kip is more bark than bite. I wouldn't worry about him too much. I heard he really wanted to be a cop but injured his back in high school, so this was the closest job he could get."

"He didn't take the job because his dad died here?" Colin asked.

Dylan pulled his neck back. "His dad?"

Colin nodded. "His dad, Doug Reynolds, died in a chemical explosion in the lab in 1974. Haven't you heard that story?"

"I—I have," Dylan stuttered. "But I didn't know Doug was Kip's dad. Small world." He paused. "You guys go head back to lecture hall. I'll be there in a minute."

"Where are you going?" I asked.

He laughed. "Do you always ask so many questions?"

"Yes," I said.

"She does," Colin agreed.

"Duly noted."

Dylan watched us as we stepped around the corner

toward the lecture hall. When we were out of Dylan's line of sight, I grabbed the back of Colin's T-shirt.

"Hey?" Colin asked.

I put a finger to my lips. "Let's follow Dylan and see where he goes." I peeked around the corner. "He's gone."

Colin and I crept down the hallway. The lecture hall was on the first floor. There were no labs on this floor of the building, only faculty offices, three classrooms, and the main lecture hall.

"I don't want to talk about this anymore," a girl's voice said around the bend in the hallway.

"I think that's Madison," Colin whispered.

I nodded and peered around the curve. Madison and Dylan sat across from each other in a small lounge outside of an administrative office.

Dylan folded his arms. "We have to talk about it."

"No, we don't. You've already talked it to death. You just need to relax. It will all go away soon."

"Other people are involved."

"I don't care." Madison made a note on her ever-present clipboard. "None of them will get into trouble. Don't worry so much."

"I have to worry. I don't know why you're not worrying. We have a lot to worry about."

"No one asked you to get involved," Madison snapped. "You begged me for attention."

Dylan's tan face turned red. The Crayola crayon box would call the color "burnt sienna." "Because I care about you. I—"

"If you care about me so much, you will let this go." She jumped out of her seat. "I have to get back to

Helium. I suggest that you return to your group too."
She stared in Colin's and my direction.

"Eep!" Colin squeaked behind me.

I reached for the classroom door behind us. It was unlocked. Colin and I dashed inside and closed the door just as we heard Madison's footsteps hurry down the hallway.

"Do you think it's safe to go back out?" Colin asked.

"I didn't hear Dylan walk by, but we have to chance it. We have to beat him back to the lecture hall."

Colin and I tiptoed in the hallway. Placing my hands on the cold brick wall, I peered around the corner. Dylan sat in the lounge with his head in his hands.

"Andi, come on," Colin hissed.

We ran as quietly as we could to the chemistry lecture.

Colin and I slipped back into the lecture hall. Dr. Comfrey was in the front of the room lecturing on bases and acids as if nothing unusual had happened the day before. Her arm was still in its blue sling and wrapped in a white bandage. A Band-Aid was on her right cheek. She smiled at Colin and me when we entered the room but didn't interrupt her lesson.

Our whole group was there except Brady, of course, and Dylan.

Colin ripped a piece of paper out of the casebook and wrote on it. When Dr. Comfrey turned her back he pushed the note across the tabletop to me.

"When are you going to talk to Dr. Comfrey?" the note read.

That was a good question. Ava watched me from the other side of the room. I crumpled up the note and shoved it in my backpack. With my luck, Ava would turn in Colin and me for passing notes. After telling Kip about seeing us with Polk, who knew what she was capable of.

Colin frowned.

"Ava's watching," I whispered out of the side of my mouth.

Colin's head whipped around in Ava's direction. "Not good."

No, it wasn't.

A second later, a new note fell on my desk. I glanced around the room for a clue of who might have tossed the note at me. No one was looking my way. I lowered the note below the tabletop and unfolded it. It read, "Hope you enjoyed your talk with Kip. – A.G."

I swallowed hard, refolded the note, and refused to look at Ava. I wouldn't give her the satisfaction.

The door near the back of the room creaked open, and Dylan stepped inside. His face was red like he scrubbed it with one of the scratchy brown paper towels from the public bathroom. His appearance made Dr. Comfrey stop talking. "Mr. White, is something wrong?"

Dylan wiped his brow. "Wrong?" he squeaked. "No, nothing is wrong."

She frowned but didn't press him further.

As class ended, Dr. Comfrey said, "Just before class, I learned I will be able to go back into my lab tomorrow morning. I'll be there bright and early tomorrow, cleaning up so that everything is ready for us to have class in that room by your class time."

"I thought Kip said that the lab was off limits," Dylan said.

She nodded. "He did, but I received a call from the police that they were done processing the scene, so I can go back inside." She held up her arm in the sling. "Since I'm a tad incapacitated, if anyone wants to join me tomorrow morning to get the lab back into order, you are more than welcome. I should be here by 7:30."

No one volunteered.

"I didn't think so," the chemistry professor said. "Okay, you are free to go to your next class."

Throughout the day, Colin and I tried to find a time for us to sneak away and talk to Dr. Comfrey, but Dylan wasn't buying any of our excuses to leave Hydrogen. Even during lunch, he made a point of sitting next to me. By the time ecology rolled around at the end of the day, I was convinced the counselor was following me.

Colin and I stomped through the woods behind the gymnasium gathering samples for ecology. Each student in our group had a list of samples we were to gather for Dr. Lime. Dylan hovered nearby, kicking over rocks with the toe of his sneaker.

"I got it," Colin said, holding a reddish-topped mushroom in his hand. "A Fly Amanita. Good thing Dr. Lime gave us these gloves to wear. These are poisonous." He dropped the sample into his net bag. "That was the one item on my list I thought I might not be able to find. I only have two more left."

Colin, as usual, was ahead of the rest of the class. Usually, I would be more competitive to find everything on my list too, but I was preoccupied by Dylan's moody behavior.

Colin held up the bag, so I could have a closer look at the mushroom. "Look how big it is. Do you want to hold it?"

I wrinkled my nose. "Maybe later. I just thought of something."

"About the toadstool."

I shook my head. "No. About Polk's situation."

He peered into his net bag, which was almost full. "What's that?"

My bag felt light. He was definitely doing better than I was. "Not counting the crickets running loose in the biology lab, have you noticed that everything that has gone wrong during camp has something to do with the chemistry lab? The missing items, the explosion."

Colin slung his net bag over his shoulder. "I had noticed that, but if someone wanted to frame Polk, that makes sense since he was a chemistry professor here."

"What if this has more to do with another chemistry professor?" I said.

Colin's brow squeezed together. "Who?"

"Dr. Comfrey, of course. She was the one who was hurt. Maybe she is the target, and Polk was the fall guy."

"Fall guy?" Colin asked.

"It's the guy who takes the blame for the crime. Bethany went through this phase a couple of summers ago where she really liked action movies. I've seen my fair share. They are full of fall guys."

Colin pushed his glasses up his nose. "It is an interesting theory, and you could be right. In fact, I think you might be."

I grinned at him. "Even I have strokes of genius now and again."

Colin blushed.

"We need to talk to Dr. Comfrey," I said.

"Okay, Hydrogen," Dylan yelled. "Let's take whatever you have back to the lab and show Dr. Lime."

As we came out of the woods, we saw the chemistry professor leaving the science parking lot in the passenger seat of a blue car. In the sun's glare, I couldn't see the driver.

"I guess we aren't talking to her today," Colin said.

My net bag of samples hung limply from my hand. "I guess not."

When Colin and I got home from camp, we found Bethany and Kaylee sunning themselves in folding lounge chairs in our front yard. Both girls wore shorts and tank tops and fiddled with their phones. "Hey, my sister is back from Camp Geek," Bethany said.

"It's not called Camp Geek," I said for the hundredth time.

Bethany waved her hand as if that were only a technicality.

Kaylee dropped her phone on her stomach. "I wish I was better at math and science like Andi. When I got my end of the school year report card, I thought my dad would blow a blood vessel over my grades. I'm lucky to be promoted to pre-Algebra. How humiliating would it be to have to take eighth-grade math freshman year?"

Bethany shivered. "I thought your dad was relaxing more about your grades."

"I'm still not living up to his Asian expectations of straight A's." She sighed.

"You're only half Asian," Bethany said.

"Yeah, but not according to my dad. He thinks my Vietnamese half should cancel out my Polish half."

Bergita whistled from her front porch. "Colin, your parents are here. They both got off early from the hospital. We are going to the steakhouse in town for dinner."

Colin's face lit up. "I'll see you later, Andi. We can talk about the case tomorrow." Colin ran across the lawn.

"But—"

He was gone before I could finish my argument. I knew Colin wanted to spend time with his parents, but we had a case to solve. We were so close.

"The case?" Kaylee propped herself up on her elbows. "What did he mean by that?"

Bethany grinned. "Andi and Colin think they are detectives. It's a boyfriend/girlfriend thing."

"Just because you don't have any friends in Killdeer doesn't give you the right to punish me because I do." I stomped past them into the house.

"She is so sensitive sometimes," Bethany said, but I heard the pain in her voice.

If I were a better sister, I would have said I'm sorry, but I wasn't.

That night, Kaylee and Bethany bounced around

my sister's room to music. Every so often, one of them would burst out laughing. I crammed my pillow over the top of my head. It didn't help.

I dropped the pillow. Mr. Rochester, who was snoozing at my feet, lifted his head and blinked at me.

"How can you sleep with all that noise?" I asked.

The orange tabby yawned.

Reaching under my bed, I pulled out the casebook. I flipped through the notes Colin and I had made over the last couple of days and turned to today's events. Colin had recorded our conversation with Kip and the one we overheard between Dylan and Madison. In the margin he wrote, "Polk never showed up on campus on Thursday."

I let the casebook fall on my stomach. Where was Polk today? I hoped he was alright.

I tapped the casebook with my pencil. Dr. Comfrey had to be the key to this case. I had to talk to her, and I knew in my gut Dylan and Madison were involved somehow too. I hated to think that Dylan pulled off any of the incidents. Madison, on the other hand, I could believe. Susan had said that Madison held a grudge. A grudge over what?

I remembered the argument I overheard between Madison and the dean about the think tank. I pictured the display case outside of the chemistry lab with the three smiling faces: Madison, Fletcher, and Dylan. Fletcher was in Washington, DC. Madison and Dylan were here. I had to talk to Dr. Comfrey.

I jumped out of bed and opened up my computer to email Colin. "Going to camp early to talk to Dr. C. You in?" I typed. I knew it was late, but I hoped he'd check his email before camp. If not, I would pound on his front door in the morning. Bergita always got up super early anyway.

Three long minutes later, Colin emailed back, "I'm in."

"Meet me in driveway at 7:20."

"Ok."

Now I just had to wait until morning. I groaned. That would go much more quickly if I was able to get some sleep.

Bethany and Kaylee shouted something, and I punched the mattress. That was it. My feet hit the blue and green rug Amelie had bought for my room. I needed to do something about Kaylee and my sister. How was I supposed to sleep with all this noise?

Mr. Rochester followed me down the attic stairs.

I placed my hand on my sister's doorknob.

"Mrs. Cragmeyer said that I could stay with her for the school year. Won't that be awesome?" Bethany asked.

I froze and listened.

"Why would you want to do that?" Kaylee asked.

"Why wouldn't I? I can go to high school with you and all my friends."

Mr. Rochester butted his head against my leg and lowered his eyelids.

"Don't judge," I whispered and listened harder, wanting to hear everything over the music.

"I think your aunt is cool, and you get to start over in a brand new place. You can be whoever you want to be here. Everyone already knows me back home. I can't change now."

"You don't want me to go to school with you?" Bethany sounded hurt.

"I do," Kaylee said. "But you should think about what you are giving up here first."

"I don't have anything here."

"You have Amelie. And what about Andi?"

"She's doesn't want to hang out with me. She spends all her time with Colin, solving little mysteries." She snorted.

I stepped back in surprise. I didn't think that Bethany wanted to hang out with me. I was the annoying little sister. I didn't know that she saw me as anything else.

"You could be nicer to her, and she would stay around more," Kaylee said.

"What do you know?"

Kaylee sighed loudly. "I'm the oldest of five kids. I know how to keep the peace."

"It's different with Andi and me."

"It should be better because you only have each other."

Because of the boy band music blaring on the other side of the door, I didn't catch what Bethany said next.

"Just think about it," Kaylee said. "Don't throw all this away to live with the Cragmeyers, whose house smells like cheese and mothballs, in case you didn't notice."

"It does not!" Bethany squealed, and their conversation dissolved into giggles.

I crept back up the attic steps to my room. Mr. Rochester was at my heels.

CASE FILE NO. 23

The next morning, I left a note for Amelie on the island in the kitchen that Colin and I were heading to camp early. My aunt wouldn't be up for another half hour. Waking her to tell her I was leaving early was out of the question because I didn't want her to ask me why.

I grabbed two packs of cold Pop-Tarts from the box and was out the door. Colin was sitting on his bike in the middle of the driveway. I tossed him one of the Pop-Tarts.

"Awesome. Strawberry is my favorite." He ripped open the silver package.

"How was your dinner with your parents last night?"

"Great!" he said around a mouthful of Pop-Tart. "We went to that steakhouse downtown. The one with the plastic bullhead sticking out of the side of the building."

I nodded.

"We ate dinner, and then afterward, Mom and Dad hung around the living room and we watched the Science Channel."

I smiled. "That's great."

"I think Bergita gave them a lecture about spending time at home."

"That's her job as your grandma."

Colin frowned. "I guess. I hope they weren't guilted into it."

"They weren't." I crumbled my Pop-Tart wrapper into the front pocket of my backpack. "Let's go. Dr. Comfrey should be in the lab by now."

Campus was quiet when Colin and I rolled our bikes through the front gate. There wasn't even a sign of Kip. I would have thought he would be lurking on campus.

We went straight into the science building and up to the second floor. Our footsteps echoed in the hallway. Light shone from the chemistry lab. Dr. Comfrey was there.

I peeked inside the lab. The destroyed Bunsen burner and glass from the explosion two days ago was swept up. The only sign of anything wrong was the burn mark on Dr. Comfrey's lab table. With the hand not in the sling, she scrubbed at the stain with a hard bristled brush, but it made no difference.

The chemistry professor looked up from the stain. Her hair was pulled back from her face in a ponytail, which only made the white bandage on her cheek stand out more.

"Andi, Colin, did you two stop by to help clean up the lab?"

Colin nodded.

"We were all too late to do it." She dropped her scrub brush. "By the time I got here this morning, everything was done, except this stain which isn't going anywhere, I'm afraid. I hate that you came out so early for nothing."

"That's okay," Colin said.

She sat at her desk and sighed at the mound of papers on it. "Look at this paperwork. You would not believe the amount of paperwork an incident like this creates."

"Does security and the police still think Polk is behind it?" I asked.

"I'm afraid so. I can't believe it myself."

Colin perched on one of the lab stools. "Who do you think tampered with the Bunsen burner?"

She eyed us. "So they told you what happened, did they?"

"Kip did," Colin said.

I sat on the edge of one of the lab stools. "Is someone upset with you?"

"Me?" She picked up her pen. "Why would someone be upset with me?"

"You were hurt in the explosion."

Dr. Comfrey stood up and walked to the first lab table. With her good hand, she opened the cupboard underneath and pulled out a box of sterile test tubes. "That is ridiculous. It's farther fetched than Kip's idea that Polk is behind all of this." She set the box of test tubes that she was holding onto her desk.

"Except for the crickets getting loose in Dr. Ruggles's biology class," I said, "everything that has happened has been directed at you. It makes me think that the crickets were just a coincidence or something to throw us off track. Is someone upset with you?" I asked again.

She frowned. "I really don't think I should be talking about this with either of you."

"What about Madison? Why is she mad at you?"

"Why do you think she is?"

"I overheard her complaining to Dean Cutter."

Dr. Comfrey pursed her lips. "You shouldn't eavesdrop, and Madison has no reason to be upset with me. If it weren't for me, she wouldn't have this job as a Discovery Camp counselor. I was the one who talked her into it."

Colin shifted on his stool. "What was she planning to do this summer instead?"

Her brow wrinkled. "She desperately wanted to go to the Chemistry Think Tank in DC. The university could only send one student, so I recommended one of my seniors. I know Madison was disappointed, but I hoped that this camp would keep her mind off of it, and she would still be able to work in chemistry." She paused. "True, being a camp counselor is probably not what she was hoping for when she planned for the summer, but it is still a good experience."

"Why didn't you recommend Madison?" Colin asked. "Did the senior have higher test scores or grades?"

She shook her head. "No. In fact, Madison is clearly the best student in the program. I chose the senior because he was a solid student as well, maybe not as naturally gifted as Madison, but someone who worked hard for his grades and studied harder. Also, he was a graduating senior and this was his last shot at the think tank. He wouldn't be eligible next summer like Madison would. She's only going into her senior year. She will have another opportunity to attend the think tank. I explained this all to Madison at the time. She's a shoo-in for next year."

"I thought you said it was suspended for next year," I said, remembering our earlier conversation.

The chemistry professor sat behind her desk again. "Yes. That was unexpected. The college has sent students to the think tank for over a decade, but university enrollment is down for next year. Every department was asked to slash its budget. I had to take funding from the think tank. It would have the least impact on the most students."

I shivered. "Does Madison know?"

She nodded. "I told her. I thought she had a right to know."

"When did you tell her?"

"The Friday before camp."

"And then markers started disappearing from the lab, and a couple days after that, there was an explosion in the lab." I pointed at her cheek.

"One of my students would never do such a thing, especially not Madison. She is my best student."

"Would Madison know how to make a Bunsen burner malfunction?" Colin asked.

"Of course she would, but so would anyone who could Google."

There was a scraping sound at the back of the lab, like someone pushed a stool aside.

Dr. Comfrey stared at someone behind me. "Polk? What are you doing here? Are you all right?"

I turned, and Polk looked terrible. There were bags under his eyes and his jowls seemed even longer than they had the day before. "Is it true? Did one of your students frame me for all of these misdeeds?"

Colin mouthed to me "misdeeds?" It was an old-fashioned word.

"Polk?" Dr. Comfrey said. "What are you doing here? The police and security are looking for you."

"I know." He dropped his head. "I was here much earlier this morning and cleaned your lab. It was the least I could do. Now I am headed to my supervisor's office to turn in my resignation. I can't work here anymore. I need to leave."

"Where have you been?" Dr. Comfrey asked. "Where were you yesterday?"

"I had to escape for a little bit. All of this has brought back so many terrible memories about Doug's death." His head snapped up. "Tell me the truth. Did your student do this?"

Dr. Comfrey pursed her lips. "We can't be sure."

I was sure. Madison had means and opportunity, and she had the best motive.

Polk shook as if he was physically holding himself back—from what, I didn't know. "I remember Doug's death every single day. Do you think I want to relive it out in the open like this? Do you think I want to be asked about it by people on campus and in town? Will I be forced to live this nightmare *twice*?" He shuddered.

"Meg, I am grateful to you for letting me pretend even for a moment that I was a chemist again, but I am not. I'm a janitor and that is all. Even that has been taken from me." He marched out the door.

Colin and I followed him.

"Polk," I said.

He held up his hand. "A long time ago, one ambitious student ruined my life, and now, it has happened again."

Dr. Comfrey stood in the doorway of the chemistry lab. Her cell phone was to her ear. "Hi, Kip. It's Meg Comfrey. Polk was just here in Colburn."

She held the phone away from her ear as Kip yelled into it.

"He is not dangerous. I am only telling you because he's upset, and I'm afraid he might hurt himself. He's extremely upset." She paused. "And you might want to talk to my student, Madison Houser. She might know something about the incident in the lab."

Colin and I shared a look and ran for the stairwell. We had to reach Polk before Kip did.

When Colin and I burst out of the building, Polk was nowhere in sight.

"How could he have disappeared so fast?" I asked.

Colin glanced back at Colburn. "He could still be inside the building."

Curie's howl broke the still quiet of the morning.

"Where did that come from?" Colin asked. "It sounded far away."

The howl came again.

"I think Curie is behind the cafeteria."

Colin and I ran across the green just as we saw Kip and two security guards stomping across campus.

Kip pointed at us. "Matt, follow them."

"Colin, run faster!" I pulled on his arm.

We followed Curie's bays.

"Hey," the guard called. "Stop!"

That wasn't going to happen.

We raced down the narrow alley between the cafeteria and library. Curie's howling was deafening now. I skidded to a stop in the small loading area behind the cafeteria. The dumpster where I spied on Kip and Polk just days ago was to my right. Polk was in front of me in the middle of the parking lot, yelling at Dylan and Madison.

A produce delivery truck blocked the only other way out. The two college students were trapped.

Polk shook his right fist. The other he had buried into his side. "How could you do this to me? Do you think of anyone other than yourself?"

Dylan and Madison stood by the dumpster. Their faces were white.

"I'm sorry. We never meant to hurt you or anyone," Dylan said.

Madison shoved him. "Shut up, Dylan. We didn't do anything."

"I can't keep lying like you can, Madison, I can't."

She stepped away from him. "Fine. I can't lie for you anymore either." She pointed to Dylan. "He did it. He did it all."

Dylan's mouth fell open. "How could you say that after everything I've done for you?"

She snorted. "What have you done other than follow me around campus like a lovesick dog?"

"Harsh," Colin whispered.

No kidding.

"You asked me to steal those things, and when I refused to mess with the Bunsen burner on Dr. Comfrey's lab table, you did it yourself," Dylan said.

Madison folded her arms. "That's ridiculous. You're trying to blame me? How dare you!"

Matt, the young guard, doubled over to catch his breath when he rounded the building. Kip and the third guard were just a few steps behind. "What's going on?" Kip demanded.

Polk pointed at Dylan and Madison. "They are the ones that caused the explosion, not me."

Madison folded her arms. "Are you going to listen to a senile old man or me?"

"Why should we listen to you, Madison?" I asked. "Because you are the best chemistry student?"

Her eyes flashed. "I am the best chemistry student this campus has ever seen!"

"And you deserved to go to the think tank this summer."

"Yes, I deserved to go! I earned it. Dr. Comfrey took that away from me. Another professor would see there are other, better ways to save money in the budget."

"So you stole items from her lab," I said, "and when that didn't get rid of Dr. Comfrey, you planned the explosion."

"She asked for it." Her mouth fell open as she realized she'd just confessed. She pointed her finger at me.

"I didn't do anything. I see what you are doing. You are trying to trick me."

A tuft of black and white fur brushed against the side of the dumpster. I pulled on Colin's arm. "It's Big Mama skunk!"

My warning came too late. Big Mama skunk turned tail and fired. It was a direct hit on Madison. The college student wailed and covered her face. I could be wrong, but I think some of the spray landed in Madison's mouth. I tried not to gag.

Colin and I took four big steps back.

"That is foul," the young guard said.

Curie howled, probably lamenting another bath to come.

Madison crumpled to the pavement and cried. Dylan made no move to go to her.

"Do you think Bergita has any hydrogen peroxide left?" I asked Colin.

Colin held his nose. "Probably. I'd use the V8 too, just to be safe."

EPILOGUE

My first day at Killdeer Middle School was two days away, and Bethany, Amelie, and I were inside the local discount store, back-to-school shopping. Colin tagged along although Bergita had bought all of his school supplies in July. She was a planner. Amelie was not. It seemed that Bethany and Amelie had reached some type of truce, and my sister was no longer asking to move back in with the Cragmeyers. I was relieved. As much as my sister drove me crazy, I didn't want to be alone out in Killdeer without her.

Amelie shook out the piece of printed computer paper in front of her. "I can't believe these supply lists. And why are there so many choices in pencils? Where are the plain yellow number two pencils? Why would you need anything else?"

Colin held up a package. "They are right here."

She grabbed two packs and dropped them in the cart. "This parent stuff is hard."

I consulted my list. "I need a calculator."

She sighed. "Don't you have one from last year?"

I nodded. "I do, but the list says I need a scientific

calculator. It's for pre-algebra." Because of my high test scores, I would be able to take pre-algebra in the seventh grade instead of eighth. Colin would be in the class with me.

"They're in the next aisle," Amelie said. "I think. I haven't bought a calculator since I don't know when. You don't have much need for one in my field."

Bethany rifled through a box of colorful folders. "This is going to take me a while. I need to decide who I want to be in Killdeer, and my folder choice is very important to my identity."

Amelie raised her eyebrows to Colin and me. "Am I supposed to understand what that means?"

I grinned. It meant Bethany was staying, I thought. My grin grew wider.

Bethany waved us on. "Go to the calculators without me."

Shaking her head, Amelie pushed the cart around the corner and nearly ran into Dr. Comfrey, pushing her own cart.

"Meg, how are you?" my aunt asked.

Dr. Comfrey smiled. "Good. Back-to-school shopping?" she asked.

I nodded.

"How's Madison?" I asked. After Discovery Camp was canceled, I never heard what happened to her.

Dr. Comfrey frowned. "She was expelled. I hated to see it happen. She was a smart kid, but someone could have really gotten hurt." She touched the bandage on her hand. Her arm was no longer in a sling. "The university really didn't have a choice. Dylan has been suspended for a semester. They both are so bright."

"Sometimes the pressure is too much," Amelie said barely above a whisper.

Dr. Comfrey nodded. "It's a shame. Dylan will be all right, and Madison will eventually get her life back together. When she does, she will apply at a new college and start over. The university decided not to press charges. There will be nothing on her permanent record, legally at least. She can start again."

"What about Polk?" I asked. "Is he back at the college?"

She shook her head. "No. He retired. It was time for him to let go of that place. In some ways he held on too long."

I frowned. "Have you seen him since he left?"

She shook her head.

Amelie frowned. "I know that look, Andi. Don't get any ideas about going to look for Polk, okay? Let the man be."

"Who? Me?"

Amelie sighed.

Dr. Comfrey laughed and pushed her cart down the aisle with a wave.

Colin held up a calculator. "Andi, you should get this one. I have the same one, and it's excellent."

I took the calculator from his hand. "It looks like it has everything I need. Since Ava will be in pre-algebra too I want the best one I can find." I tossed it into Amelie's cart.

"What's next on the list?" Amelie asked.

"Tomato juice," I said. "Considering this summer, I think we need to stock up."

"Don't forget the hydrogen peroxide," Colin added with a grin.

We laughed, and I felt ready for my new school and new school year, whether Ava Gomez liked it or not.

ACKNOWLEDGEMENT

When I wrote this book, I was under the greatest stress and pressure of my life, so the novel is aptly titled. During that time, it was a welcome relief to escape into Andi's world of mystery and middle school hijinks. I have many people to thank for allowing me this creative getaway.

I'm grateful to my agent, Nicole Resciniti, who cares about me enough to know when I need her to be my career advocate and when I just need her to be my friend. I am also grateful to the editorial and middle grade teams at Zondervan, including Mary Hassinger, Britta Eastburg, and Sara Merritt, for their support and creativity, as well as Kim Childress, my first editor for Andi. Kim knows Andi as well as I do.

Thanks to Dr. Sarah Preston, chemistry professor and friend, for answering my tireless questions and helping me find the right explosion that was "big but not too big." Any mistakes in the novel are mine alone.

Love to my friends and family, who support me through the many changes in my writing career, especially Andy, Nicole, Isabella, Andrew, Delia, Mari-ellyn, Meredith, and Suzy.

Andi Under Pressure will always have a special place in my heart because it is my last novel my mother, Rev. Pamela Flower, read before she went home to heaven. Even at the end of her life she pushed me to be a better writer and a better servant for God. She was the perfect mother for me and the best friend I will ever have.

Finally, thank you to God in heaven. May everything I write be pleasing to you.